Ru~~ffle~~

Dune House Cozy Mystery Series

Cindy Bell

Copyright © 2015 Cindy Bell

All rights reserved.

ISBN-13: 978-1522747048

ISBN-10: 1522747044

More Cozy Mysteries by Cindy Bell

Dune House Cozy Mysteries

Seaside Secrets

Boats and Bad Guys

Treasured History

Hidden Hideaways

Dodgy Dealings

Suspects and Surprises

Ruffled Feathers

Sage Gardens Cozy Mysteries

Birthdays Can Be Deadly

Money Can Be Deadly

Trust Can Be Deadly

Ties Can Be Deadly

Rocks Can Be Deadly

Jewelry Can Be Deadly

Bekki the Beautician Cozy Mysteries

Hairspray and Homicide

A Dyed Blonde and a Dead Body

Mascara and Murder

Pageant and Poison

Conditioner and a Corpse

Mistletoe, Makeup and Murder

Hairpin, Hair Dryer and Homicide

Blush, a Bride and a Body

Shampoo and a Stiff

Cosmetics, a Cruise and a Killer

Lipstick, a Long Iron and Lifeless

Camping, Concealer and Criminals

Treated and Dyed

Table of Contents

Chapter One

Gray stretched out before Suzie. The overcast morning left the ocean without its sparkle. Suzie wrapped her arms around herself in a light hug to block out the morning chill. She loved the moments just after dawn when only the fishermen were out and the quiet was only interrupted by the crash of the waves against the sand. It was not long ago that she had taken a leap and changed her life. She could honestly say that it was the best decision of her life. The shared responsibility of Dune House with her best friend, Mary, had brought a sense of purpose and freedom that she hadn't expected. After one last deep breath of the crisp, salty air Suzie turned and walked back towards the majestic house.

It was a grand, old house, and its many rooms welcomed guests from all over the world who wanted the quaint bed and breakfast experience that Dune House offered. When Suzie first inherited it, it needed a lot of work and remodeling. Now, it was once again the gem that shone over the town of Garber. Suzie was almost to the side door that led through the dining room when she noticed a shadow along the exterior wall. She paused and watched as the shadow became more defined. From the distance where she stood she could see the outline of a figure. Suzie narrowed her eyes.

Although Mary did wake up early she tended to stay in the house or sit on the porch. She did not think that it was likely that Mary would creep around the side of the house. Suzie began to follow the shadow. In her past as an investigative journalist she always had a knack for spotting trouble. This looked like trouble. She walked around the side of the house and saw the back of a man's head. He leaned heavily on the wall and attempted to peer through the window of one of the first floor bathrooms.

"Excuse me? Just what do you think you're doing?" The man straightened up and turned to

2

face her. She recognized him right away. "Maurice? What are you doing?" Maurice lowered his eyes.

"I'm not doing any harm. I promise that, Suzie."

"You can promise it all you want, but that doesn't explain why you're peering in one of my bathroom windows."

"No one's in there."

"Thank goodness. What are you doing?" She raised an eyebrow.

"I just wanted to see if that beast had arrived yet."

"Beast?" Suzie shook her head. "You're not making any sense. Did you forget your meds today?"

"Ha ha." Maurice jabbed his thumb towards Dune House. "You've got Priscilla Kane staying here. I know you do. How could you let her stay?"

"I have no problem with Priscilla."

3

"Well, you should." He crossed his arms. "Her plans are going to affect all of us."

"Maybe. Maybe they will change things for the better. Why a person stays at Dune House is not my business. If they want to book a room, they can have a room, and they are welcomed just like any other guest."

"I think that you need to be more concerned about the way that things are going for this town. The locals have accepted you, but that can change."

"Are you threatening me, Maurice Lungdley?" Suzie's bright blue eyes squinted at the corners. "Because that's a very dangerous thing to do."

"No, I'm not threatening you. I'm warning you. No one is going to be happy about you allowing her to stay here. It's going to ruffle some feathers."

"I don't care if people are unhappy, I can let whoever I want to stay, stay. It's my bed and breakfast."

"Don't say I didn't warn you."

"Not that it's your or anyone else's business, but she has not arrived yet. She will arrive today. If I see you or anyone else hanging around here trying to cause trouble I will make sure that Jason is notified so the police can handle it. Understand?"

"Oh sure. It must be nice to have a cousin with a badge. You can grand stand all you want, but you know as well as I do that if this development happens in Garber our perfect little seaside town will be destroyed."

"Maurice, go back to your motel and take care of your guests. Stop worrying so much about things you can't control." Suzie waved her hand through the air and headed for the door. She looked back once to be sure that Maurice walked towards the parking lot. As she stepped into the dining room her heart did flutter a little. Priscilla Kane was someone who held a lot of power, and she knew it. She and her business partner, Neil Runkin, were due to arrive later that day for check-in. Although Suzie did believe in what she had said to Maurice she couldn't deny that she was a little anxious about Priscilla's arrival.

"Morning. I made us some coffee." Mary smiled as Suzie walked into the kitchen. Suzie took a moment to admire her friend. Though Mary was completely unaware of it she was a pretty woman with soft features and loose, auburn hair just touched with gray. She was only a few years older than Suzie.

"How are you this morning?" Suzie leaned against the counter.

"Not too bad. My knees are just a little stiff, but not too sore today."

"Oh good." Suzie smiled and accepted a mug of coffee.

"I'll be even better once I loosen up a bit." Mary winked at her. "I have to be. Wes is going to take me out tonight to one of his favorite restaurants, it's German."

"Oh, that should be delicious."

"I'm looking forward to it. I already checked in on Priscilla and Neil's rooms, they are all set."

"Thanks Mary. You will not believe who was lurking around outside."

"Who?"

"Maurice Lungdley."

"Oh wonderful. So it begins." Mary shook her head. "We're not going to be the most popular people around here for allowing them to stay here."

"Maybe not, but I think we did the right thing. I don't have to agree with someone's views or their intentions for them to have a room at Dune House."

"I know." Mary sighed. "I just hope that she'll decide against using Garber as the location for her new, all-inclusive resort."

"People will still want to stay in a quaint bed and breakfast."

"I know, it's not that. It's just that Jude's Café

7

will become a chain coffee outlet, and the diner will be turned into a fast food place. It's just hard to watch it happen."

"Our town is strong enough to make it through."

"Maybe," Mary said. She gazed down into her cup of coffee. "I guess we will find out."

***

Suzie walked through the dining room, the living room, and the front lobby to make sure that everything was as it should be. It was easy for things to get out of place when they had multiple guests. She straightened a few pillows and turned on some accent lamps to give the living room a cozy feel. Even though Dune House had been quite a surprise in her life she had come to love it. It was almost as if she never had a home until she settled there. Perhaps Paul was part of that, too. Just when she was certain that she would never need another companion he appeared in her life.

As Suzie stepped out onto the deck off the

dining room to check on the seating there, she caught sight of a patrol car pulling into the large parking lot. Suzie pushed one of the chairs up against a metal table then brushed her hands off. She walked out to the parking lot just as a young man stepped out of the patrol car. In uniform Jason should have looked older, but to Suzie he always looked youthful.

"Morning Jason."

"Hi Suzie. I just wanted to stop in and see how everything is going."

"Fibber. You're here because you know that Priscilla Kane and Neil Runkin are arriving today."

"Okay, maybe." He smiled. "I just want to make sure that no one is hassling you."

"I'm fine, Jason." She thought about mentioning Maurice, but she didn't want to cause the man too much trouble. She knew that he was desperate to protect the future of his business and she assumed that he was harmless.

"Good. Well, you know I'm just a phone call away."

"I know." Suzie nodded.

"Is Paul in yet?"

"No, not yet."

"Can you let me know as soon as he docks?"

"Sure. Is everything okay?"

"Yes, there's just something I need to talk to him about."

"Okay, no problem." Suzie smiled at him. "Thanks for checking on me."

"Always." He smiled then climbed back into the car. As he drove away Suzie was reminded of how sweet it was to have family. When she returned to the bed and breakfast Mary met her in the dining room.

"Was that Jason?"

"Yes, he came by to check in on us."

"Aw, how sweet."

"It was." Suzie grinned. "Priscilla should be here in a few hours."

"I checked in on Stewart, he's doing well and is going on a boat tour later."

"Oh good. He's so quiet, one of the best guests we've ever had."

"I think he just prefers to be left to his own devices, which certainly makes our job less stressful."

"Yes, it does," Suzie agreed. "I don't think Priscilla Kane will be quite as easy."

"Nor do I. Her reputation is not exactly known as being low maintenance."

"Well, we'll be ready for her." Suzie walked towards the front desk. "As long as she has everything she needs then she should be just fine."

Mary nodded in agreement. "I'll take one more look in their rooms to make sure everything is just right."

"Thanks Mary."

Chapter Two

As Suzie sorted through the paperwork at the front desk she thought about what they might face when Priscilla and Neil arrived. It was not exactly the easiest thing to deal with a demanding guest, but they were getting used to it and Suzie felt it would be worth it. If Priscilla and Neil were well taken care of she hoped they would mention it to their associates and that could draw more guests to Dune House. As she finished up the front door of Dune House swung open.

"Hello hello? Is there someone who can get my things?"

Suzie looked up with surprise. Priscilla Kane stood in the doorway with a large birdcage in one hand and a tiny glittering purse in the other. It looked like it was encrusted with diamonds. The same extravagance was reflected in the outfit she wore which was as colorful as it was expensive. Priscilla appeared to be in her early fifties, but

13

Suzie knew that she was closer to sixty. She became interested in Priscilla when she found out that she was planning on building a resort in Garber and was staying at Dune House.

"Ms. Kane, I apologize, I didn't expect you so soon. I will go and get your things for you."

"Never mind that, just get me checked in. You can get my things once that's settled."

"That will just take a moment." Suzie pulled up Priscilla's file on the computer and began entering in her arrival information. "Your room is all prepared for you. Breakfast is included with your stay. We can also provide lunch and dinner if you let us know. I've booked the room across the hall for your business partner."

"Oh dear, I'm not sure that I need to be that close to Runkin."

"I can switch his room if you'd like." Suzie did her best to conceal her surprise. She assumed that they were friendly since they had booked the same place to stay, but working together and staying

14

together might have become tedious. So far Priscilla's visit was not going very well.

"It's fine. I'm sure he'll keep himself occupied with the most expensive things he can. What time is dinner tonight?"

"At six, but if you need to come later you're welcome to. Dinner is available until seven-thirty."

"That's very flexible of you. I'm sure I will have no problem being there by six. I'm going to take a little nap. The drive was a bit much for me."

"Of course."

"Please make sure that there is no draft in my room as I would not want my Benita to get sick." She smiled at the bird through the bars of the cage.

"We'll make sure." Suzie assured her. She peeked in through the bars of the birdcage at the parakeet. "She's beautiful."

"Yes, she is. She talks, too." Mary walked up to the desk as Priscilla continued to rave about her

15

bird. "Although, sometimes I wish she didn't repeat so much." She rolled her eyes. "Let me tell you it's caused some rather awkward moments."

"Really?" Mary's smile widened. "I always wanted a bird as a pet."

"Oh no, no. She's not a pet. She's my family. It's very important to me that she is well taken care of, understand?"

"Yes, of course." Suzie smiled to assure her. "We will treat her as if she is another guest."

"Thank you." Priscilla sighed with relief. "Some people don't understand, but Benita is the closest family I have."

"I'll show you to your room if you would like." Mary gestured down the side hallway.

"I'll go and get your things." Suzie walked around the desk.

"Wonderful." Priscilla smiled.

"Here, let me get Benita for you." Mary reached for the cage.

"No, no. Only I carry my Benita. Thank you." She picked up the cage and followed after Mary. Suzie stepped outside to find Priscilla's driver waiting beside the trunk.

"Where can I place these?" He adjusted his cap.

"If you'd like you can take them right into Priscilla's room."

"No, I'm sorry. I'm not allowed to do that."

"Why not?" Suzie picked up one of the suitcases. It was not heavy.

"Priscilla prefers that not many people are allowed into her living areas. When I drive her home I may leave things in the foyer, but I may not actually enter any further into the house."

"Isn't that a little strange?"

The middle-aged man lifted his shoulders in a mild shrug. "When you work with the very wealthy you get used to strange. I'd be happy to take them into the lobby for you."

17

"No, that's quite all right. I'll take them in. Are you staying nearby?"

"Yes. A motel." He nodded. "I will be available to Ms. Kane whenever she needs me."

"All right." Suzie picked up the other suitcase which was also fairly light.

"There's one more thing." He hauled out a hard shell overnight case. When Suzie tried to take it from him she nearly fell over. It was heavier than both of the suitcases. "Bird seed."

"Ah." Suzie nodded. "I'll come back for that." She carried the suitcases to Priscilla's room. She arrived just as Mary stepped out.

"Oh, Priscilla wants to take a nap and not be disturbed until dinner."

"Okay, I just have one more bag to bring in." Suzie hurried back to the front of Dune House just in time to see another car pull up. It was a flashy, bright orange sports car, the kind that she had only seen in the movies or on the cover of magazines.

"Here's Neil." Priscilla's driver grinned. "That's my cue to leave." He climbed into the car and drove off just as Neil opened his car door. He was a tall, clean-cut man. He appeared to be in his forties, the suit he wore was as simple as it was immaculate.

"Hello." He nodded to Suzie who struggled to hold on to the small, but very heavy bag.

"Hello, Mr. Runkin, welcome to Dune House."

"Ah, I see that Priscilla remembered the bird seed." He grimaced. "She's always afraid that Benita is not getting enough to eat. No one seems to be able to get through to her that Benita is a bird not a person."

"Some people do consider their pets to be family."

"Sure." He wiggled his eyebrows. "Family."

"Right this way, Mr. Runkin, I'll be with you in just a moment." She led him into the lobby, then left him at the front desk as she carried the last bag to Priscilla's room. Mary passed her in the hallway.

"Neil Runkin has arrived, can you check him in for me?"

"Absolutely." Mary held the door open for Suzie and cringed as Suzie heaved the bag into Priscilla's room. Priscilla was already settled in her bed with a sleep mask to shield her eyes. Suzie hurried out of the room to avoid disturbing her. However, before she could pull the door closed behind her the bird in the cage began to shriek.

"Nuts! Nuts!" Suzie shut the door with a shake of her head. "I hope she packed some ear plugs, too."

***

Suzie arrived at the desk just behind Mary. Neil was standing at the desk and before they could say a word he looked at Mary and started talking.

"Good afternoon. I'd like a wake-up call, turn down service, and I will not be having dinner here."

Mary smiled. "Well, good afternoon to you, too, Mr. Runkin and welcome to Dune House."

"Yes, yes. I know all of what you intend to say. Please spare me and just show me to my room."

"As you wish." Suzie stepped forward and nodded. "We can settle the paperwork later." She led him to the room across the hall from Priscilla's. "Priscilla Kane's room is just across the hall," Suzie said as she pointed to the door.

"Oh good. I'll be sure to look in on her. Thanks." He pushed the door closed behind him. Suzie stood outside the door for a minute. She was accustomed to showing the guest around the room and answering any questions they might have. Mary met her at the end of the hallway.

"I guess Neil isn't the friendly type," Mary said.

"Yes, Priscilla was downright warm compared to him." Suzie and Mary walked back to the front desk.

"It certainly seems that way."

"Although, apparently Priscilla does have some strange ways according to her driver, but she did seem very nice. She didn't ask for much at least."

"That's true." Mary frowned. "That doesn't change how the town is going to receive her though."

"I'm afraid that you're right about that. However, I hope that we can still show her a good time."

"I still think we should be careful about how friendly we get with Priscilla. Suzie, you know if the deal goes through we're going to have to choose a side." Mary straightened some paperwork on the desk. "It doesn't pay to be neutral."

"I didn't expect this from you, Mary." Suzie leaned against the desk.

"It's not just about what we feel, Suzie, it's about how we show our support to the community. If the town doesn't want the resort, and we show support to it, then the town is not going to want to support us."

Suzie sighed. "I guess you're right about that. We'll have to keep a close eye on things."

"Wes warned me that things could get ugly. He's seen things like this create huge feuds in the community and residents become violent. He's even seen the meetings erupt into the street."

"I think that's a little extreme."

"I guess that we'll see." Mary straightened up.

"That's it for check-ins, right?" Suzie peered at the appointment book.

"Yes, unless we have any last minute guests. We have a light load over the next few days. Wes and I are going to go to German tomorrow night instead of tonight so I'll be here for dinner. I thought that we can have the leftover beef stew from yesterday and I'm also going to try a new soup. Do you think that will be all right?"

"Yes, of course I do. I love your creations."

23

"Wonderful. I'll just get some of the vegetables ready. Let me know if you need anything."

"I'm going to take a quick walk around the grounds to check on things, then I'll be back in."

Suzie stepped out through the front door. She noticed that there were several cars passing Dune House. They drove slowly, but sped up when she appeared on the porch. Suzie looked towards the small town of Garber. The main street was lined with tiny, privately owned shops. The library was well-stocked but small. Even the police station was just large enough to look imposing. There was nothing grand about Garber, aside perhaps from Dune House. She tried to picture the massive resort, stretched along the majority of the beach. Maybe some would consider it progress, but she couldn't imagine Garber being any other way than it was now.

When Suzie stepped back inside she was greeted by the heady scent of soup. The flavorful aroma tickled all of her senses.

"Oh Mary, that smells delicious!"

"I think so, too." A man's voice drifted out of the kitchen. Suzie walked towards it.

"Wes? Is that you?" Suzie asked.

"It is." Wes smiled and started to speak again, but his mouth was occupied when a spoon was thrust towards it.

"Try it now, I added a few more spices," Mary said.

Wes savored the soup with a deep moan. "I don't think it can get any better, Mary."

"Well, you're wrong, it just needs to simmer a little while longer and then it will be perfect."

"I could get used to home-cooked meals." Wes licked his lips. "Microwave dinners can't compare now that I've tasted this."

Suzie eyed the pair as they shared a quick kiss. It warmed her heart to see such affection between them, but it also worried her just a smidgen. She hoped that Mary wouldn't be in any rush to set up house with Wes. They might not have known each other terribly long, but they were quite comfortable with one another.

"Are you joining us for dinner tonight, Wes?" Suzie peered into the soup pot.

"No, I'm afraid I can't. I'm due at work in half an hour." Wes was a detective in the neighboring town of Parish.

"I'm making him a container to take with him." Mary smiled. "And some rolls, some stew, and some dessert."

"Aw." Suzie winked. "You're spoiling him, Mary."

"I don't mind." Wes grinned. "Though my waistline is starting to pay the price."

"You're perfect." Mary patted his stomach.

"Thanks." Wes' cheeks flushed.

"I'll leave you two lovebirds alone and set the table. Did any of the guests opt in for dinner?"

"Just Priscilla. I haven't heard a peep out of

Stewart, and Neil made it clear that he will not be eating here."

"That's fine, more soup for us." Suzie winked. She carried the dinner service tray out to the dining room table. As she set the table for three she could hear Mary and Wes chatting in the kitchen. A subtle squeeze in her chest reminded her that she missed Paul. It was a new feeling for her to long for a man. She smiled at the thought that he would be back soon. Sometimes the time away made the reunion that much sweeter. Once the table was set Suzie started back towards the kitchen. Mary and Wes passed her in the entrance.

"I'm just going to walk Wes out to his car."

"Okay. Good night, Wes."

"Night Suzie. Enjoy the soup. I know I will." He held up a brown paper bag. Suzie smiled and ducked into the kitchen.

As Suzie washed a few of the dishes that Mary had used while making the soup she considered what a conversation with Priscilla might be like. She didn't have to wait long to find out as Priscilla walked into the dining room a few minutes later with Benita in her cage.

"I'm sorry, I know I'm early, but I just couldn't wait any longer. I've been absolutely tortured by that scent. It is so divine."

"Well, there's no reason why we can't have dinner a little early. It will just be the three of us."

"Four!" Priscilla held up the birdcage with a smile.

"Oh yes, of course, four." Suzie smiled.

While Suzie settled Priscilla at the table Mary began to serve the soup, along with bread, and a homemade cheese spread. Benita's cage was perched on the chair right next to Priscilla.

"Would you like some wine?" Suzie offered.

"No, thanks." Priscilla shook her head and then tasted a spoonful of the soup. "Oh, this is delicious. What is that flavor?"

"Ginger." Mary smiled. "It's a new recipe I wanted to try. I hope you enjoy it."

"I do, very much." Priscilla dipped her spoon back into the soup. "I'm so glad that I decided to stay here for dinner. Neil insisted on making a reservation at some five star place in Parish. I just have a hard time enjoying restaurant food over and over again. It's really been a long time since I've had anything home-cooked."

"Mary's meals are always delicious." Suzie raised her glass of wine to her friend. "I promise you, you will never leave the table hungry."

"Speaking of hungry," Mary said. "I'll just dish up the stew." She stood up and started spooning the stew onto three plates.

"Thank you! This is like a feast," Priscilla said as Mary placed a plate in front of her. "I have to say that I didn't expect such a warm welcome."

"Oh?" Mary sipped her wine.

"No, I've done this many times you know. I like to find small towns so I can help them grow.

In each and every town there is resistance. This is the first time I've been treated like a guest rather than an invader. I really appreciate that."

"Well, we're very happy to have you." Suzie smiled. "Our first priority is providing a comfortable, warm environment for our guests."

"I'll have to remember that motto for the resort. Too many people these days forget that a vacation is actually supposed to be a vacation with as little work as possible."

"That's the truth." Mary nodded. "We have some guests who arrive here with every minute of their vacation mapped out from start to finish. It amazes me that they aren't more exhausted from their vacation than their regular work schedule."

"I don't know, I've always enjoyed a good adventure." Suzie gazed out through the double glass doors that led onto the deck. She wondered what kind of adventure Paul was having out there on the water. She enjoyed boats and she wanted to join him. "But I also love the quiet nights curled up in front of a fire with a good book."

"Oh yes." Priscilla sighed at the idea. "That I do love. Thank you, ladies, for the company, I guess I should turn in."

"There are books in the living room if you'd like to pick one out." Mary smiled.

"How lovely." Priscilla picked up the birdcage.

"Nuts! Nuts!" The bird squawked.

"You'll have to excuse her, she gets a little excited." The bird continued to squawk as Priscilla disappeared down the hall. Suzie and Mary exchanged a look over the remainder of their stew.

"I guess that Benita is more of a fan of nuts than ginger," Suzie said.

"Must be." Mary grinned.

Chapter Three

The next morning was a busy one. Suzie prepared breakfast, while Mary tidied the rooms. Priscilla appeared in the kitchen just as Suzie stacked up a platter full of french toast.

"Oh, that looks tasty!" Priscilla said as Neil stepped into the kitchen behind her.

"You're not really going to eat that are you?" Neil scrunched up his nose at the french toast that Suzie had prepared. "It's loaded with sugar."

"It looks fantastic to me." Priscilla smiled. "If you want to starve that's your choice. I'm going to get a good breakfast under my belt before we start our community tour."

"Fine, fine." Neil sat down beside her and reluctantly accepted a plate.

"Thank you, Suzie." Priscilla smiled at her as she picked up a fork, ready to dive in.

"You're very welcome." Suzie offered a warm

touch to the woman's shoulder. Then she turned her attention to Neil. "I can assure you, Neil, I didn't put too much sugar on the toast."

"Sure." He pushed the toast around his plate.

"Runkin, don't be so rude." Priscilla rolled her eyes. "If it isn't made by a chef on television he thinks it isn't worth eating."

"Well, I can tell you that I've never been on television, but this is my favorite kind of french toast. Mary taught me the recipe."

"I'm eating, aren't I?" Neil shoved a forkful into his mouth. Suzie did her best not to be insulted by the grimace that swept over his face.

"I wondered if you two might like a list of some of the attractions in town."

"No thanks. We have a plan." Neil cleared his throat. "Can I have some water please?" Suzie nodded and gave him a bottle of water.

"Yes, we have a few places we're going to visit before we head to the community meeting. Will you be going, Suzie?"

"I don't know." Suzie frowned. "I'm not sure that it's the right place for me to be."

"Well, I'd love to hear your opinion, plus you'll have a chance to learn more about our plans. I hope to see you there," Priscilla said.

"Thanks." Suzie smiled. She joined them for breakfast and kept a plate warm for Mary. Mary and Stewart walked into the kitchen a few minutes later.

"Is there any french toast left?" Stewart looked hopeful.

"Yes of course, I'll get you a plate," Suzie said. After giving Stewart the french toast they ate in silence.

"We should be going." Priscilla finished the last bite, then wiped her mouth with a napkin. "Thanks for breakfast, Suzie, and I hope to see you later. Both of you." She nodded to Mary as she stood up. Neil followed after her though he did not bother to say goodbye. Suzie began clearing the breakfast dishes.

"I can do that." Mary started to stand up.

"No way, you've just cleaned the rooms, rest a bit. Then you can keep me company while I wash the dishes."

Once everything was piled into the sink Mary joined Suzie in the kitchen.

"I can't get over how different Neil and Priscilla are. I do hope that Priscilla does most of the talking at the meeting."

Suzie sloshed a sponge through the soapy water. "I think we should go to the meeting."

"Suzie, I don't know if that is a good idea. We are hosting Neil and Priscilla, our presence there might be taken the wrong way."

"That we are interested in Garber and supporting its citizens?" Suzie stacked a few dishes in the drainer. Mary promptly picked them up and began drying them.

"Or that we support Priscilla and Neil which is not something that we can do if we want to keep the support of the locals."

"We are the locals now, Mary. I think we've been here long enough to call ourselves that. I'll be honest, it really bothered me how aggressive some people were towards us when we first started renovating Dune House. I think it would be nice to show Priscilla and Neil some courtesy." Suzie washed the last dish and handed it over to Mary.

"Suzie, are you telling me that you can't see the difference here?" Mary stared at her for a long moment.

"Tell me, Mary. What am I missing?" Suzie studied her friend. She trusted Mary's opinion above any other opinion. There was no question that they had lived different lives, but they had always been able to advise and guide each other through the bumps and valleys. Mary could always make Suzie's thoughts clear for her.

"Suzie, this isn't the city. When we came here people were upset because they expected Dune House to go to Jason, they also expected it to remain untouched. Even though they had no

36

ownership of Dune House, they considered it their own, a part of their hearts. But we won their trust by respecting the environment, the history of Dune House, and using only locals to help us with the construction. Priscilla isn't planning to do any of that. She's planning to drop a giant resort on the small amount of beach property that is available here. It will block the view for many of the locals, it will put many of the shops out of business, and it's not likely that they will use any local help to build it. There have been numerous studies that show the impact on the wildlife will be atrocious, yet Priscilla doesn't appear to care. That's the difference. You and I rebuilt Dune House with love and respect, Priscilla just wants to own a chunk of the beach and make as big a profit as possible."

Suzie pursed her lips and nodded a little. "I guess you're right. Sometimes I think the people around here are too resistant to progress, but I forgot, this town only exists because it creates and supports its own economy. A huge resort would disrupt everything."

"Not to mention the fishing." Mary shook her head. "Wait until Paul gets in and finds out who we have staying here. I dare say he will not be happy."

"I didn't even think about that." Suzie cringed. She hadn't mentioned the guests to Paul only because it never occurred to her to, but she hoped he wouldn't think that she had deliberately hidden it from him.

"More watercraft, more people, more tourists, more pollution, pretty soon this won't be a fishing town anymore." Mary sighed. "I've seen it happen in many small towns, and I can understand why people don't want it to happen here."

"I never really thought about all of that. In the city new businesses popped up all the time and it didn't have much of an impact on the city. But this is different."

"So, do you still want to go to the meeting?" Mary put the last dish on the shelf.

"Yes. Yes I do. I want to show support for the town, even if it has to be silent. I don't want to pretend I don't know what is happening."

"Okay, then I'll be right there beside you," Mary said.

"Great. We'll leave around two? The meeting is at two-thirty."

"Perfect, I'll be ready."

Suzie walked back to her room to straighten up. When she stepped inside she caught sight of a photograph of Paul on her dresser and paused. The ocean was a part of Paul. He would be devastated if the beach or the wildlife in the area was damaged by a development. In that moment she understood why the people of Garber were so angry. It wasn't just about their income or economy, it was about their passions and their sense of peace being shattered, all for the sake of bright beach umbrellas and jet skis.

***

When it was time to leave Suzie met Mary on the front porch of Dune House.

"Any word from Neil or Priscilla?" Suzie glanced over the empty parking lot.

"They haven't been back. They must be going straight to the meeting. Do you want to drive?"

"Yes." Suzie held up her keys and gave them a brief shake. "You know I like to be behind the wheel."

The two friends drove into town to the municipal building which housed some conference rooms that the locals could reserve and use. When Suzie tried to find a parking spot there were very few to choose from.

"It looks like the meeting is having a big turn out."

"There's one." Mary pointed to an empty spot. Suzie managed to park the car in the narrow space.

"Let's get inside before there's no room left." Suzie led Mary down the hall towards the room that the meeting was scheduled to be held in. The door was open and voices spilled out into the hall. The meeting hadn't started yet, but it seemed like the majority of Garber was in the room. Mary made her way inside, and Suzie stepped into the packed room just behind her. She recognized many of the people in attendance, but not all. She saw Maurice at the front of the room with his shoulders raised and tight.

"Standing room only." Mary glanced over her shoulder at Suzie.

"We can fix that." Suzie tapped the shoulder of a young man seated in the back row. "Hello there." She smiled at him. He looked at her, then at Mary and nodded.

"You want to sit down?"

"My friend here would like to," Suzie said.

"Yes, ma'am." He nodded and stood up without an argument.

"Suzie, you didn't have to do that." Mary frowned.

41

"Mary, very few perks come with age, we should take advantage of at least a few of them."

Mary nodded with appreciation and settled into the chair. "Thank you." She smiled at the young man who leaned against the wall. A moment later the meeting began. Suzie noticed that the entire row was filled with private business owners. She cringed as she thought of what Priscilla would face. Neil stood beside her at the front of the room, but their attitudes couldn't have been further apart. Neil's broad shoulders were tense, his eyes hooded, and his lips curled up in a mild sneer. Priscilla smiled at every person she made eye contact with, and appeared enthusiastic. When the meeting was turned over to her to give her speech she stepped up to the microphone with a bounce in her step.

"Hello everyone, my name is Priscilla Kane. I know many of you have done your research on me, but you should know that I am not the person that the media depicts. Yes, I am wealthy, but I am not alone in that. The towns I have worked with before have become wealthy as well, along with many of their residents. We want the people of Garber to know that what we are offering isn't just a resort. It's guaranteed jobs, a place on the map, and the opportunity for small business owners to truly flourish."

"That's not true!" Maurice shouted. He rose to his feet, as did a few other people in the room. "I've researched these other little towns that you've been to. All you do is destroy them. You hire outside help, you systematically replace small businesses with chain stores and franchises. If you build this monstrosity you will destroy Garber."

Several shouts erupted from the crowd in support of Maurice's words.

"Now please, just try to calm down. That doesn't have to happen here. If we work as a team to get this project on its feet then the entire community will benefit." Although her words were calm and soothing, it was too late. Half of the conference room was on their feet. A moment later Jason's voice rose above the din. Suzie hadn't even seen him come in, but he was there, just when trouble brewed, as always.

"That's it! The meeting is over. Everyone needs to clear out," Jason said sternly.

"It's not over!" Maurice glared at him. "It's not over until these people leave our town once and for all!"

"It's over when I say it's over, Maurice!" Jason stepped in front of him and fixed a steady glare upon him. "One more word and I'll walk you out of here myself."

Maurice opened his mouth to speak, but Jason held up a finger. Maurice closed his mouth. Jason waved people out of the room. Suzie and Mary were swept out the door along with the crowd.

"Good thing Jason was there." Mary clutched her purse. "That could have gotten ugly."

"Yes, it could have." Priscilla paused beside them. "I guess there is a lot of anger against the resort. Hopefully we'll be able to turn that around." Mary looked down at her shoes. Suzie summoned a smile to her lips.

"I'm sure that you will be able to. You might want to consider some of their concerns," Suzie said.

"Oh, yes of course I will. But first I'm going to make it clear that I have not been scared off. Suzie, I really don't want to run off and hide. I'd like to be seen in the town after this horrible meeting. Is there a place I could go for dinner? Somewhere that the locals dine?"

"I think Cheney's is always a great place to go. It has delicious food and the staff are always friendly."

"That sounds great." Priscilla met her eyes. "Hopefully the people will be welcoming."

"You might get a few glares or looks, but in general you should be able to enjoy a meal. If not, you can always come back to Dune House and have some dinner."

"Great. I'll keep that in mind. I will see you later this evening." As Priscilla walked away Suzie turned towards the parking lot. She almost walked right into Neil. He didn't bother to excuse himself. In fact he didn't look at her at all. He held his head high and ignored the sneers and comments of the locals as he walked past them. Suzie watched as he walked towards his car. He didn't seem the least bit phased by what happened at the meeting.

"That was wild," Suzie said as Mary fell into step beside her as they headed to the parking lot. "Maybe we never should have gone."

"No, I think it's important that we were there. Now we know what we are dealing with," Mary said as she pulled open the passenger side door. "And so does Priscilla for that matter."

"Neil didn't seem to mind." Suzie rolled her eyes. "He marched around as if he was the king of Garber."

"I wonder if either of them even plan on living

here. Priscilla mentioned that she's done this in several different places. Why would they care what damage they do to the town?"

"You may be right, Mary. I hate to think that about Priscilla as I actually kind of like her, but there's no arguing the fact that the community does not want this resort."

"So? Do you think that Priscilla will bow to the pressure?"

Suzie started the car. "No Mary, I don't think that she will. In fact she didn't even appear to be flustered by what happened tonight. If she is used to this kind of reaction then she probably has numerous ways to deal with it."

"And you think that we should just sit back and let her do that?" Mary gazed out the window. Suzie saw Dune House rise up before them.

"Yes. I think we should let her have her say. The worst it can do is pull the community together against a common enemy."

"Or we could end up with a monstrous resort."

Suzie parked a few feet away from the front walk and turned the car off. "It's possible. But what can we really do, Mary? It's not as if we can throw them out on the curb, that would be worse for our reputation and they would only find someplace else to stay. If we remain neutral, we'll get the up-to-date information about the deal, and we can decide what to do then."

"Okay."

The bed and breakfast was quiet when they walked in. If Neil was there, he was silent, as was Stewart. However, Benita squawked loudly through the door of Priscilla's room.

"I don't think that bird ever sleeps." Mary shook her head. "If you don't mind, I'm going to take a nap. I have a date with Wes tonight and I'm already exhausted."

"I don't mind. Get some good rest, Mary." She gave her friend a quick hug.

When Suzie stretched out on her bed to read some of her book she could still hear the angry voices of the people at the meeting. They echoed through her thoughts, and made concentrating on the plot line quite difficult. She left her room and checked to see if any of the guests had signed up for dinner. Since none had and Mary was going out she decided to have some leftover soup. She took it out onto the side porch to eat. As she watched the waves rush and retreat she wondered whether Priscilla would have her way in the end. Could Garber really be consumed by one development deal?

Chapter Four

The next morning Suzie woke very early. It was too early to even prepare breakfast for the guests. She decided to take a walk along the beach. In just her socks she made her way through the house to avoid waking any of the guests or Mary. She tugged on some slip-on shoes by the door and opened it. When she stepped out onto the porch she drew a breath of the salty air.

"Morning!"

Suzie jumped and gasped. She spun around to see that Mary sat in one of the rocking chairs. "Mary, you scared me."

"I'm sorry." Mary laughed. "You should be proud of how high you can jump."

Suzie laughed as well. "I thought you were still sleeping."

"No, I guess that nap was too much for me yesterday. I've been up since five."

"How was dinner last night?"

"Amazing." Mary smiled and gazed out at the water. "Never in a million years did I think I could feel this way about a man. Well, you know what I mean."

"Huh?"

"You and Paul."

"Oh sure, I enjoy his company."

"You enjoy his company?" Mary grinned. "That's one way to put it."

"How would you put it?"

"Maybe you're in love." Mary stood up and stretched.

"I love how things are. I certainly wouldn't want them to change."

Mary caught her eye and her smile grew a little. "There's only one thing in life that doesn't change, Suzie."

"What's that?"

"The fact that everything changes."

51

"Oh, thanks for that!" Suzie rolled her eyes and laughed.

"It's true." Mary chuckled.

"Want to go for a walk? It's too early to put out breakfast."

"Sure, I'd love to." Mary smiled.

Suzie hooked her arm through Mary's and the pair walked down the slope of the side of the property to the beach. It was that sleepy time of morning that was filled with only the wonder of the expansive sea. As they walked along the beach a few of the locals began to emerge from their beach houses. Friendly waves were exchanged, but no one spoke, the crash of the waves was sacred. They walked towards the pier. Mary paused to pick up a seashell nestled in the sand. When she stood back up she gasped.

"What is it Mary? Are you hurt?" Suzie grabbed her arm.

"Oh no, it's Priscilla! Suzie, it's Priscilla."

"What do you mean?" Suzie followed her gaze

to the water. As the waves lapped at the sand Priscilla's body rocked back and forth. Suzie lunged forward and grabbed Priscilla's wrist to check for a pulse. When she couldn't find one she placed her cheek close to Priscilla's lips, but again there was no sign of life. In fact it was fairly evident that Priscilla had been dead for some time.

"Mary, call Jason!"

"I already am." Mary's hand shook as she held the phone against her ear. "Jason, you need to get here now, Priscilla Kane is dead."

Suzie searched the sand and water for any clue as to what might have happened. Priscilla certainly hadn't gone for a swim. She was fully clothed right down to her high heels. Suzie's mind raced. She hadn't seen Priscilla come back in the night before, but she hadn't expected her to. Maybe if she had stayed up late enough she might have noticed the woman was missing. Sirens screamed through the air shattering the quiet morning. People on the beach stopped what they were doing and looked towards Mary and Suzie.

"Mary, we have to make sure no one gets too close. Who knows what might have happened."

"I'll take care of it." Mary nodded. She walked towards the people that approached. Jason and his partner, Kirk, raced across the beach towards Suzie with medics close on their heels. A few other officers jogged behind them. When Jason stopped beside Suzie he looked from her to the body.

"What happened?"

"I don't know. We just found her like this. I checked for a pulse and breathing, but she's gone, Jason." One of the medics looked at Jason and shook his head sullenly to confirm that she had passed away.

"Are you okay?" Jason met her eyes with concern. "You should sit down."

"I'm okay. I just can't believe that this happened. Do you think someone killed her?" Jason's attention returned to the body. He crouched down beside it and began looking it over.

"Hmm, I don't see a mark on her. At least not visible." Jason peered more closely at the body.

"Looks like she might have just fallen off the end of the pier into the water. Poor woman." Kirk shook his head. "It's a shame."

"Is that what you really think?" Suzie frowned and crossed her arms. "I find it hard to believe that she would just slip. Why would she have been so close to the edge? Even if she fell in, why didn't she swim to shore?"

"She had all of her clothes on. Plus the water is very deep at the end of the pier." Jason sighed as he looked out over the water. "People, especially tourists, have no idea how powerful the waves and the pull of the ocean can be. She probably panicked. It was dark, she was scared, she might have even swum in the wrong direction. I've seen it before."

"Yes, there's no evidence of physical harm, her clothes aren't torn that I can see. No visible head injury. Jason's right. She likely plunged in and was too shocked or disoriented to get to shore. We'll get the medical examiner to do an autopsy of course, but at the moment this is considered an accidental death." Kirk shoved his hands into his pockets and growled under his breath. "The media is going to love this. After that meeting yesterday and now this, it's going to be a circus."

"First we need to get in touch with her family, then we'll worry about the media." Jason looked up at the crowd of people that began to gather. The other officers kept them back. "What's Mary doing?"

"She was keeping everyone away. We don't want photographs of Priscilla ending up splashed across the internet."

"Good thinking, Suzie. Thank you." Jason gritted his teeth. "I'm sorry to do this to you when you've had such a shock, but I do need to ask you a few questions."

"Of course." Suzie nodded.

"Do you have any idea what she was up to last night? Did she mention anything to you?" Jason looked back out over the water.

"I suggested that she should have dinner at Cheney's. She wanted to be seen by the community. I thought Cheney's was a good place." Suzie frowned. "I'm not sure if she made it there or not."

"Did she mention if she was meeting anyone?"

"No, I'm sorry. It was just a brief conversation. Like I said, I don't even know if she went there."

"Well, let's find out." Jason nodded to Kirk. "See if you can get hold of any of the employees that were working last night. Let's find out if she might have had a reaction to something, or maybe she had too much to drink."

"Okay, I'll do that now." Kirk walked away while dialing a number on his cell phone. Mary made her way back to Suzie and Jason. Suzie wrapped an arm around Mary's shoulders.

"Are you okay?"

"I think so, Suzie. I just can't believe that she's dead."

"It's a shock to everyone." Jason took off his hat and ran his hand back through his hair. "I'm not sure how she could have ended up here. Mary, did you notice anything strange about her yesterday?"

"No, she seemed fine to me."

Kirk walked back towards them, his features shadowed. "According to a member of the staff at Cheney's, Ms. Kane had quite a bit to drink. Then as she left the restaurant she stumbled. I got the time of departure."

"Wow. Maybe she was so drunk that she took the wrong path. She probably thought she was headed back to Dune House and instead she was on the pier. It must have been too late once she fell into the water. She was too drunk to keep her

58

head above water." Jason clucked his tongue.

Suzie and Mary stepped away as the two continued to discuss the death. Mary looked over at her.

"What is it, Suzie?"

"Hmm?"

"I know that look."

Suzie sighed. "I just don't think it could be true."

"What isn't true?"

"Well, Priscilla getting drunk and walking off the pier. She was so put together. She actually came across as rather warm to me. She also didn't seem like someone who would be so reckless."

"You may be right. People hide their addictions well though."

"But she didn't even ask for wine at dinner." Suzie narrowed her eyes. "It just doesn't make sense to me."

"I'm sure if something is suspicious about it,

Jason will figure it out."

"I hope so."

Chapter Five

By the time Suzie and Mary got back to Dune House there was no sign of the guests. They had missed breakfast, but there were no angry notes left behind. Suzie stood beside the kitchen counter and tried to think of what to do next. She was so shocked by the discovery that she couldn't get her thoughts straight. Mary leaned against the counter beside her.

"We should see that Neil is okay and make sure he knows about Priscilla's death," Suzie said. Mary bit into her bottom lip. "Don't you think he should know?"

"Yes. And I would hate for him to come to us about something before he's been informed," Mary said. "I wonder how he will take it. We should see him together. Is that okay?"

"Yes, let's just get it done, the longer we let it go the harder it will be." As they walked down the hall towards Neil's room Suzie tried to think of how to break the news. At Neil's room she knocked on the door. Mary grimaced as they waited for him to open the door. After a few moments, Suzie knocked again. Again there was no response.

"Maybe he's already out for the day?"

"Maybe." Suzie frowned. She turned away from the door and looked straight at Priscilla's room. "What about her things, Mary? I think we should get them together for her family."

"Oh, how horrible this is going to be for them. To think one night of too much drinking took her life."

"I don't know," Suzie said. "I still don't think that's what happened. Maybe I am just too paranoid, but it all seems rather strange to me."

"Hopefully we'll know the truth eventually." Mary turned the knob on the door. "It's locked." She reached into her pocket for the keys that she always carried with her. She slid the key into the lock.

"Wait." Suzie touched her arm. "Let's just be careful when we go in. Maybe this was an accident, but something tells me that it might not have been. Jason may not need to search the room now, but if anything changes there might be evidence in here that they will need to recover."

"Good thinking." Mary opened the door. Right away the bird began to squawk. Mary walked over to the cage and lifted the cover. The bird hopped from ledge to ledge and bobbed its head anxiously. "It's okay. It's okay." Mary clucked her tongue. "Poor birdie."

"Look at this." Suzie picked up a ream of paperwork that was on the top of the dresser. "Looks like she was working hard." She started to open the folder.

"No don't. Like you said, let's leave everything just the way it is, just in case there's a problem. Other than the bird of course, we're going to have to keep her with us until someone claims her."

"I'll check for any dirty linen." Suzie opened

the hamper in the closet. She was surprised to find it empty. She checked the shelf in the closet for the stack of three towels they always made sure was in each room. There was nothing on the shelf. Suzie opened the door to the small bathroom in the room and looked around. There were no towels in there either. "Did you put towels in this room, Mary?" Suzie asked as she stepped out of the bathroom.

"Yes, of course."

"Well, they're not here now. They're not in the hamper either."

"Maybe she left them in the main bathroom?" Mary said referring to the large shared guest bathroom for the floor. It had a larger shower and a bathtub.

"Maybe. I'll go check."

Suzie left Mary in the room and walked down the hall to the shared bathroom for the floor. When she reached the linen closet beside it she realized that the carpet beneath her feet was soaked. She frowned as she tried to track down where the water came from. The rest of the hallway was dry. The patch of carpet between the linen closet and the bathroom was wet. She opened the door to the bathroom and found puddles of water on the tiled floor. The towel rack was empty. Mary met her outside the door.

"What went on here?"

"It looks like one of the guests took a shower and didn't have a towel. They must have stood in front of the linen closet to find one," Suzie said.

Mary opened the door to the linen closet. "Hm. It does look like a few towels are missing."

"I'm sure they will turn up in a wet pile in someone's room." Suzie shook her head. She knew people had different standards of cleanliness, but she hated the idea of wet towels getting moldy somewhere.

"I'll clean this up. Why don't you take the bird to the front desk? That way she will be ready when someone wants to pick her up and we can keep an eye on her."

"Sure." Suzie walked back to Priscilla's room. She picked up the birdcage and carried it to the front desk. "Here you go, don't worry I won't be long." She whistled at the bird then walked to the utility closet. She pulled out a wet dry vac that could draw the water out of the carpet. As she carted it out of the closet and down the hall the bird began to flap her wings and shriek a word.

"What is that you're saying? Pumpkin?" Suzie raised an eyebrow. The bird shrieked again. The closest word that she could think of was pumpkin. "Okay, well I don't have any pumpkin." She shook her head and continued down the hall to the bathroom. Mary finished hanging up some fresh towels in the bathroom and turned to look at Suzie. "Oh perfect, thank you," Suzie said.

"No problem. I want to make sure this is all cleaned up before any guests return. This day is already upsetting enough I don't want any slip and falls."

Once the bathroom was cleaned up Suzie was restless. Her mind kept returning to Priscilla and what might have happened to her.

"You know what I think, Mary?"

Mary stuck her head out of the kitchen. "What?"

"I think it's been far too long since we visited Dr. Rose. In fact we've been downright neglectful for not stopping by to check in on our friend."

"I think you're right." Mary smiled. "We should remedy that with a visit right now."

"I agree, Mary. We owe her a serious apology."

Mary picked up her purse and followed Suzie out the door. They drove towards the medical examiner's office. Suzie searched the sidewalks and the cars she passed for Neil but she didn't see him or his vehicle. When they reached the medical examiner's office Suzie parked as close to the door as possible. She knew Jason would not appreciate the fact that she was checking up on the case

67

without his knowledge so she wanted to be able to make a quick exit if she needed to. She and Mary hurried inside and were greeted by an empty waiting room. There was no receptionist at the desk. This did not surprise Suzie as Dr. Summer Rose liked to work alone and would often give the office staff the day off if she didn't think it would be a busy day.

"Maybe we should go." Mary glanced around.

"No, I'm sure she's in the back, let's just take a peek." Suzie walked towards the double doors that led out of the waiting room.

"Suzie wait, do you think we should go back there?"

"Dr. Rose?" Suzie stuck her head beyond the double doors. A medicinal scent stung her nose as she took a breath.

"I'm back here, Suzie." Her soft voice drifted from behind a second set of double doors. Suzie and Mary walked through both sets of doors to find Summer bent over a clipboard on her desk.

"Sorry to interrupt." Suzie paused a good distance from a curtain that she knew was drawn around Priscilla's body.

"It's fine," Summer said.

"I got your message." Jason's voice drew all of their attention as he walked into the room. His eyes met Summer's for a long moment as they both smiled at each other. "Suzie, Mary!"

"We just wanted to say hello to Summer, since we were passing by," Suzie said quickly before Jason could question why they were there. She didn't want him to think they were trying to find out information about the death behind his back, even though they were.

"Really?" Jason said in disbelief. "Well, it's good that you're here. I think you might need to hear this." He looked at Summer.

"I have to say this is one of my most surprising and frustrating cases." Summer sighed.

"An accidental drowning?" Mary raised an eyebrow.

"I wish," Summer said. "That's what it was supposed to be, but there's a few problems with that assessment."

"Was she dead before she went into the water? No water in her lungs?" Suzie asked.

"Oh, there's plenty of water in her lungs, but she was definitely dead before she went into the water, for the second time."

"What?" Jason narrowed his eyes. "What do you mean?"

"As I expected she drowned, however, when I tested the water in her lungs it was not salt water."

"That doesn't make any sense." Mary frowned.

"No, it doesn't. It appears that she drowned elsewhere and ended up in the ocean. Which means that unless she drowned, got up and walked to the ocean, someone moved her body. So, we are at the very least looking at someone moving the body, but judging by some of the bruises that have begun to arise on her skin, it was a homicide."

"So, someone drowned her somewhere else and then dumped her in the ocean?" Mary cleared her throat. "That is horrible."

"Yes, it is. Unfortunately, because of her being in two different kinds of water for a long time there is little to no DNA evidence remaining on her body, or her clothes." She gestured to the plastic bag of Priscilla's clothing. Suzie looked at them through the plastic. She noticed that one of the shoes had a broken heel.

"Did you notice this, Summer? Her heel is broken."

"I did."

"Maybe that was why she stumbled out of the restaurant." Mary snapped her fingers. "She wasn't drunk, she stumbled because she broke her heel."

"Yes that's possible. Although there was alcohol in her system it was nowhere near the level that would cause severe intoxication. I think

71

we can safely say that she was maybe a little tipsy, but nothing more than that. Also, we are waiting for more results, but preliminary tests show there were no drugs in her system. In fact Priscilla was quite healthy for her age." Summer sighed as she looked up at Jason. "I'm afraid I'm not going to be much help on this case. That's why it's frustrating. Now that we know that it's likely a murder I'd love to find some evidence, but even her fingernails have been washed clean from being under the water. I have no idea if she attacked the person who killed her. I wish I had more to go on."

"Are you able to tell where the water came from?" Jason asked thoughtfully. "Maybe that would give us a clue."

"I am getting some tests run on it, which will take time. The best way to tell is to have a sample to compare it to. Pinpointing the exact location is going to be difficult because most of the evidence has been washed away by the extended period of time in the water."

"Extended?" Suzie looked over at her. "How

long do you think she was in the water?"

"Oh, at least eight hours. I'm placing the time of death around nine or ten. Maybe a little later, maybe a little earlier."

"So, a while after she left the restaurant," Jason said. "We are going to need to ramp up our investigation. It's officially a homicide, which means we're going to need to search her room, speak to everyone she had contact with, including you Suzie, and Mary." He patted the curve of Summer's shoulder. "Thanks for the quick catch on this. We've already lost a lot of time."

"I wish I could tell you more, Jason," Summer said.

"I might have something of interest." Suzie frowned. "There was someone snooping around Dune House the day that Priscilla checked in."

"Who?" Jason turned to face her. "Why am I just hearing about this now?" His voice tightened.

"Wait a minute, this morning this was an accidental death, nothing more, why would I mention it?" Suzie said defensively.

"Maybe because I stopped by to specifically check on you?" Jason raised an eyebrow.

"Look, Maurice is a businessman, I understand why he was upset. I didn't think too much of it, but now, I don't want to hold anything back about it."

"Maurice Lungdley, the same man that I had to escort out of the community meeting?"

"Yes. I can't see him doing this, but I thought you should know."

"Thank you, Suzie. I appreciate that." He sighed. "If you think of anything else, please don't hesitate to tell me. This entire case is going to turn into a big mess once word gets out that it's murder. At least I have somewhere to start. Maurice Lungdley." Jason spun on his heel. "I'd better get over there and find out where he was last night."

"Be careful, Jason, he can be temperamental," Suzie called out.

"Don't I know it. Have you seen Neil Runkin? We've been trying to get hold of him all morning." Jason shook his head.

"He wasn't at Dune House this morning."

"Well, let me know when you do see him. I want to speak to him."

"Sure," Suzie said. Jason paused at the door and looked back at Suzie.

"Don't forget to let me know when Paul gets in. Okay?"

"I won't forget." Suzie smiled.

After Jason left, Mary looked over at Suzie. "What's that about?"

"Who knows? Maybe they're trying to bond?" Suzie shrugged.

Summer laughed. "I'd like to be a fly on the wall for that."

"Me too." Mary stifled a laugh. She glanced at her watch. "Oh dear, we'd better go check on Benita, maybe her food has run out and she's hungry."

"I also want to see if Neil is back yet. It seems odd that he hasn't heard of Priscilla's death yet and come to Dune House to sort things out."

"Maybe he did and he doesn't know how to handle it. He doesn't seem like a man who is too in touch with his emotions."

"I can agree with you on that." Suzie rolled her eyes. "Let's check up on Stewart, too. He's been awfully quiet."

"Good idea. When he gets wind of all of this it might spook him."

Chapter Six

As Suzie and Mary drove back to Dune House, Garber appeared more somber. Suzie wondered if word had already gotten around about the true cause of Priscilla's death. She knew that in a small town like Garber bad news spread fast and scandalous news spread like wildfire. When they pulled into the parking lot at Dune House Suzie noticed that Neil's car was still not in the parking lot. She and Mary walked up to the door and stepped inside. It was uncomfortable for Suzie to think about the woman who would never collect her luggage or her beloved bird.

"I guess he's still not here."

"I'm going to make us some lunch. We didn't even have breakfast."

Suzie nodded. "I'm not sure if I can eat."

"You're going to have to. It's important."

"I know, I know." Suzie frowned. She walked

over to the front desk as Mary disappeared into the kitchen. Suzie picked up the phone and dialed the number for Stewart's room. After the third ring he answered.

"What is it?"

"I'm just checking in to see if you are doing okay today."

"Ah, because of Priscilla?"

"You've heard."

"Who hasn't?"

"I want to assure you that everything is being done to find the person responsible."

"I'm sure it is. But I have to say that this doesn't feel much like a vacation anymore. I'm going to check out tomorrow morning."

"I'm sorry to hear that. I wish your departure was under better circumstances."

"It's quite all right. I've enjoyed my visit here, but I don't want to be caught up in the middle of a murder investigation. It's a shame, a real shame."

"Yes, it is. Please let me know if there's anything I can do, or anything you might need."

"Thank you. I won't be attending dinner tonight. I have plans to meet someone for dinner."

"Okay, thank you, Stewart."

"Thank you, Suzie. Don't worry, I intend to visit again."

"Great." Suzie sighed with relief as she hung up the phone. The last thing she needed was a bad review spread throughout the community because of something that she had no control over.

"Pumpkin! Pumpkin!"

"Ugh." Suzie rolled her eyes. "All right, all right. I'll feed you." Suzie walked over to the birdcage and opened the door to refill the food dish. As she filled it she heard footsteps approach from behind her.

"What's Benita doing down here?"

79

Suzie turned around to find Neil dressed in the same clothes that he wore the day before. "Neil, have the police contacted you?"

"The police? No. Why would they?"

Suzie frowned. "Neil, I'm sorry to be the one to tell you this, but Priscilla Kane has passed away."

"Has what?" Neil's eyes widened. "She's dead?"

"Yes, I'm sorry for your loss."

"Are you sure?" His brows knitted together and Suzie thought for just a moment that he might begin to cry. Instead he shook his head. "I didn't think anything could kill that woman." Suzie raised an eyebrow. That wasn't exactly the reaction she expected.

"We're taking care of her bird until we're able to contact family. Unless of course you would like to have Benita with you."

"No, absolutely not. That feathery beast never quietens down." He scowled at the bird. The bird flapped its wings at him. "So, what was it? A heart attack or something?"

"No, I'm afraid she drowned."

"Drowned? She didn't even like to swim, that I knew about. Well, I guess I didn't really know if she liked to swim or not."

"No, she didn't drown while swimming. She was intentionally drowned. Neil, she was murdered."

"Murdered?" Neil took a step back. His face grew pale. "Are you sure about that?"

"Yes, Sir." Suzie reached for a box of tissues. "If there's anything that Mary and I can do to help, please don't be afraid to ask."

His face grew red as he glared at the box of tissues. Instead of grabbing a tissue his eyes fluttered as he looked away. He grabbed the edge of the front desk to steady himself. "Am I in any danger?"

"I don't believe so. Why would you think that?" Suzie grabbed his elbow to steady him.

"Well, if someone killed Priscilla I'm guessing it was someone from around here, someone who wanted to stop the resort from being built. They might be after me, too. Don't you think?"

"I'll tell you what, I'll call my cousin, he's a police officer. He can give you a better idea of whether you might be a target."

"Oh sure, local police. No, I think I'll be hiring a bodyguard until I can get out of this town." He narrowed his eyes. "I'll be checking out first thing in the morning."

"I'm sorry to hear that, Neil, but I certainly understand. In the meantime if there is anything that you need please feel free to ask."

"What could I possibly need from you?" Suzie watched as he walked away. "Someone in this backwards town is going to pay, I promise you that." She heard him slam the door to his room. The abrupt sound caused a shiver to race along her spine. Maybe Neil didn't know how to express his grief, but he certainly knew how to express his anger.

"Suzie, lunch is ready!" Mary stuck her head out of the kitchen to get her friend's attention. Suzie, still a little startled from Neil's behavior, joined her friend in the kitchen.

"Well, I just told Neil what happened," Suzie said as she walked into the kitchen.

"Oh? Was that the slam I heard?"

"Yes. I don't think he was the least bit pleased. He seemed just as angry as he was upset."

"People react to things differently." Mary placed a grilled cheese with freshly sliced tomato on the bench in front of Suzie. All of a sudden Suzie was hungry, very hungry.

"Oh, that reminds me, I'd better let Jason know that Neil is here." She sent Jason a text. After a few bites of her sandwich she heard a knock on the door, then the door swung open.

"Suzie?" Jason called out as he stepped into the lobby. Suzie stole another bite of her sandwich then excused herself.

"Jason, you got my text?"

"Yes. Is Neil still here?"

"Yes, he is in his room. Room six."

"All right." He walked down the hall towards the room.

"Jason, he didn't take it well."

Jason spun on his heel to look at her. "You already told him?"

"Yes." Suzie frowned. "Is that a problem?"

"I would have liked to see his initial reaction myself. So yes, it is a bit of a problem. I wish you had waited until I arrived."

"I'm sorry, Jason, I thought he should know as soon as possible," Suzie said. "He was wondering why Benita was downstairs and I couldn't lie."

"It's all right." Jason sighed. He knocked on the door of Neil's room. There was no response. Jason knocked again. Again there was no response.

"Are you sure he's here?"

"I didn't see him leave." Suzie stepped past him and tried the door knob. The room was locked. "Neil?" She knocked on the door. "Neil, are you in there?"

Jason frowned when there was no answer. "Can you open it?"

"Sure." Suzie pulled the keys out of her pocket and unlocked the door to the room. When the door swung open the room was spotless, and also empty. The bed was made and the furniture was neatly arranged. Jason started to step inside.

"Jason, what are you doing?"

"I was just going to take a quick look around."

"No."

"What?" Jason turned to look at her.

"Neil's my guest. I can't just let you into his room."

"You did unlock it for me." He crossed his arms.

85

"Yes, but that's because I thought Neil might be hurt. Not to let you snoop through his things."

"Really? You're going to lecture me about snooping?" Jason laughed.

"Jason. I'm serious."

His smile faded as he looked at her. "Suzie, Neil could be involved in this. I might be able to find a lead if I look around."

"Do you have any reason to suspect him?"

"None. But business partners are often involved in disputes. Are you really going to deny me the chance to find evidence?"

"We don't even know where Neil is. I didn't see him leave."

"He must have slipped out when you weren't looking. Where he is doesn't matter as much as why is he sneaking around?" Jason peered at a pile of papers on a table.

"Jason." Suzie frowned. "I'm not comfortable with this."

"I'll remember that the next time you want me to give you information about someone." He raised an eyebrow.

Suzie sighed. "All right, fine. But you know as well as I do that anything you find without a warrant can't be used against Neil."

"Why would anything be used against me?" Neil stood in the hall just behind Suzie. "Why are you in my room without my permission?"

Suzie cringed.

"I was looking for you, Mr. Runkin, to discuss the murder of Priscilla Kane," Jason said as he stood tall and walked towards him.

"Are you accusing me of something? What right do you have to be in my room?" Neil glared at Suzie. "Did you let him in here? You did, didn't you?"

"I thought you might be hurt." Suzie frowned. "I thought you were inside and not answering."

"Oh, now you have so much concern for your guests? Where was that concern when Priscilla was missing all night?" He chuckled. "And look who's here. Junior Deputy Dogood."

"Junior what?" Jason narrowed his eyes.

"You want to look around my room without a warrant?" Neil stepped into the room with Jason. "Feel free. I have nothing to hide. Priscilla and I were business partners, that's it."

Suzie's stomach churned as she watched the two men face off. She couldn't help but feel that she was somehow responsible for the fireworks of tension between them.

"Why don't we start with you telling me where you were last night?" Jason pulled out his notebook.

"I wasn't here." Neil shrugged. "I was being entertained by a lady friend."

"A lady friend? It wasn't Priscilla?"

"Please." Neil scowled. "After the meeting I met a woman on the beach, and well, she appreciated my plan for the future of Garber."

"What was the name of this woman?" Jason looked up from his notepad.

"You really think I'm going to tell you that so you can smear her reputation? No. I have no reason to tell you who I was with. I was not here, and I was not with Priscilla. That's all that you need to know."

"So, you're not interested in cooperating with this investigation?"

"What I'm not interested in is dealing with a small town cop who has no idea what he is doing. For all future contact you can go through my lawyer. If you don't mind I'd like you to leave my room. I need to pack."

"I'll be in contact with you soon, Mr. Runkin." Though Jason's tone was polite Suzie could see the squint of his eyes and the tension in his jaw. He stepped out of the room. Neil promptly closed the door behind him. They both heard the click of the lock. Jason gestured towards the living room. Suzie followed after him. He did not speak until they were outside on the porch together.

"That guy is a real piece of work."

"Yes, he is." Suzie folded her arms across her chest.

"I'm sorry that I've gotten you into a problem with him. But I do think there's good reason to suspect him. He refuses to give an alibi."

"He did come back today with the same clothes he wore yesterday," Suzie paused. "Actually, he must have changed between the time he came in and the time we saw him. His clothes were different."

"Interesting. Maybe he took a shower. That might have been why he was not in his room."

"His hair wasn't wet."

"Maybe he didn't wash it." Jason shrugged. "Either way, I'm going to see about getting a warrant. I want to know what is in his room that he didn't want me to see."

Suzie nodded. "I'll keep an eye out."

"Please do." He started to walk away, then stopped and turned back. "No Paul yet?"

"Probably not until tomorrow. Is everything okay, Jason? You've been asking about him a lot."

"Sure, everything's fine." Jason glanced away.

"What is it?"

"Nothing Suzie."

"Is it about me?" Suzie's heart dropped.

"It's nothing bad, Suzie." Jason smiled at her. "At least I don't think it is. I just need to talk to him when he gets in, all right?"

"All right." Suzie waved to him as he walked to the parking lot.

Chapter Seven

A few hours later Suzie was so restless that she decided it was time to do some investigating of her own. It was the only way she could get herself to calm down. She paced back and forth through the living room as she began to carve out a plan.

"Suzie?" Mary nearly collided with her as she walked into the living room. "Are you okay?"

"Yes, I think so. Neither Neil nor Stewart has signed up for dinner, so do you want to go out for dinner tonight?"

"Wes is taking me out to dinner again tonight. Do you want to join us instead?"

"No, thank you." Suzie smiled. "I'll be back by eight."

"Okay, I won't be." Mary grinned. "I'm hoping we will go for a walk after. Although, we might just avoid the beach."

"I don't blame you for that. Have fun. I will be on call in case any of the guests need anything. All right?"

"Great. See you later, Suzie."

"See you later." Suzie stepped out of the front door of Dune House and walked over to her car. With every step she took she had a strange sensation that something might just pop out at her. She looked around the property a few times, but didn't notice anything strange, aside from a window that was off track. She tried to tug it back into place, but it was wedged. She made a mental note to ask Paul for help with it when he docked.

When Suzie arrived at Cheney's it was as busy as ever. Suzie swept her gaze over the wait staff in search of familiar faces. Though she didn't often dine out, when she did it was usually with Paul at Cheney's. She had also become familiar with the employees from the restaurant and from running into them from time to time in town.

"Melissa!" Suzie waved to a young waitress

who had just walked away from a large table of diners.

"Suzie." She smiled as she walked over to her. "Where's Paul?"

"A table for one tonight I'm afraid. Anything good on the menu?"

"Everything's good on the menu." Melissa winked at her. "Just a minute and I'll get you a table by the window."

"Thanks, Melissa."

As Suzie waited for her table she noticed a familiar face in the crowd. It took her a moment to remember who he was. Priscilla's driver. He glanced over at her, but didn't seem to recognize her. Then he settled in at the bar. Suzie walked over to him and leaned against the bar beside him.

"Can I buy you a drink?"

He looked up at her. "Sure, I guess. You're from the bed and breakfast, right?"

"Yes. I'm sorry about Priscilla."

"Yes. That was a shock. My boss wants me to wait here until the matter is settled, so I'm staying."

"In the motel right?"

"Yes."

"I know the owner. Is he taking care of you well?"

"Sure, I guess. Clean towels, a working television, what more can you ask for?"

"I'm Suzie by the way. I don't think I caught your name."

"It's Conner."

"Conner, did you notice anything strange happening around the motel?"

"Strange?" He shrugged. "You mean other than the people?"

"What was strange about the people?"

"Just you know, some seedy types."

"Sure." Suzie nodded. "Anything other than that? Maybe someone arguing or something?"

"There was some arguing about money. I don't know who it was though. It sounded like two guys. I didn't see either of them, I was in my room. But I could hear them out in the parking lot."

"Did you tell the police?"

"No reason to. I didn't think it had anything to do with Priscilla, still don't. They didn't mention her or anything."

"What about family?"

"Look, I don't know anything about her. All I did was drive, and like I said, she was private. I didn't get to know her."

"All right." Suzie glanced towards Melissa who signaled to an empty table. "Thanks for your time, Conner."

"No problem." He returned to his drink. Suzie didn't think he was telling her everything. She settled at the table and ordered a glass of wine. As she relaxed into her seat she studied the others gathered in the restaurant. It was eerie to think that Priscilla had her last meal in the restaurant, if she even ate. When Melissa returned with Suzie's wine, she placed her order for ravioli. Then she gestured to the empty chair across from her.

"Can you sit for a minute?"

Melissa glanced around at her tables, then plopped down in the empty chair. "Just for a few minutes."

"Melissa, do you remember serving Priscilla Kane last night?"

"Sure. It's crazy that she died. I mean, I was just talking to her."

"Did you notice anything strange about her last night? Was she upset?"

"Not at first. She came in, I seated her, then I seated her friend."

"Her friend? She was dining with someone?"

"Yes."

"Did you tell the police that?"

"Well no. No one asked. It was busy when they

97

questioned us so I guess that it just slipped my mind."

"Do you know who he was?"

"No, it wasn't a he. It was a young woman. And when they first sat down they were cordial to each other. I took their order, but before I could even bring them their food, they started arguing."

"Just a little back and forth?"

"No it was more than that. Raised voices. Slammed silverware. I was close to tossing them out."

"Did you hear what they were saying?"

"Not really. Something like, you don't understand, you're too young to get it. Then the young woman went on this rant about how Priscilla was selfish, how she couldn't ever see past herself, and that would never change. Then she stormed out."

"Are you sure there was nothing else?"

"No, I'm sorry."

"What about payment? Did the other woman pay for the check?"

"No, Priscilla paid for all of it. She left not long after that."

"Was she drunk?"

"She had some drinks, but I think she was more upset than drunk."

"Did you see her leave?"

"Yes, she kind of stumbled out the door." Melissa glanced back at the big table. "I'm sorry I have to check in on them."

"It's no problem, you've been very helpful." Suzie made a note on her napkin about the woman who shared a meal with Priscilla. At the very least she was someone to look into.

When Suzie finished her meal she left payment and a tip on the table and walked towards the door. She noticed that Conner was still at the bar. He nursed a beer, but kept his eyes on the door. Suzie looked towards the door just in time to see Neil step through it. He didn't notice

Suzie, but walked right up to Conner. The two spoke too quietly for Suzie to hear. She frowned as she continued out the door.

It seemed rather interesting that Neil, who only liked fancy places and people would go out of his way to a small Italian restaurant, and speak to a lowly driver. As Suzie drove back to Dune House she wondered whether Mary's night had been pleasant. She hoped that it had. When she parked she saw that Dune House was dark, but for the two lights that they always left on. The porch light and the living room light. That either meant that Mary was home and asleep, or still out with Wes. Suzie made her way into Dune House through the front door. She knew that Neil would not be there, and she presumed that Stewart would be tucked away in his room. As she walked through the living room towards the front desk she heard a subtle flutter.

"Pumpkin! Pumpkin!"

"Oh dear, not this again." Suzie paused in front of the cage. "What's wrong, Benita, are you hungry?" She made sure the bird's water and food dish were full. But the bird continued to shriek. "Pumpkin! Pumpkin!"

"Hmm, something tells me you like Halloween." Suzie shook her head. "I can't have you keeping our guests awake. I guess you will have to come with me." She picked up the cage and carried it into her room. She set the cage down on a table near the window. Then she draped a thin blanket over the top of the cage to get the bird to settle down. In the silence that followed she took a deep breath. She knew that Paul would be getting in sometime the next day. She looked forward to seeing him, but she couldn't be too excited with the weight of Priscilla's death hanging over her head. Who was the woman she met with in the restaurant? Why was Neil so cagey?

Chapter Eight

When Suzie woke the next morning the first thought on her mind was Paul. He would be arriving at any time that day. She smiled at the thought. The second thought was about Priscilla and what might have happened to her. She decided that the most important thing was to find out who was having dinner with Priscilla the night she died. That person might be the only person that knew exactly what happened to Priscilla. From what Melissa said she assumed the woman was much younger than Priscilla. She decided that she would attempt to ask Neil about her. She dressed and then headed for the front desk. She knew that both Stewart and Neil planned on checking out that morning. Mary already had coffee brewing.

"Did you get in late last night?" Suzie smiled at her.

"Quite late. Actually, I do have something to

tell you."

"What is it?"

"Wes and I decided to walk through town instead of on the beach. We bumped into Carl, you know, he runs the pharmacy? Anyway, we started talking about the tragedy of Pricilla's death. He mentioned that he had seen Priscilla, and another woman, walking through town together."

"Really." Suzie raised an eyebrow. "Melissa, the waitress at Cheney's told me that Priscilla ate with a woman the night of her death, but she said they argued."

"According to Carl they walked arm in arm. He noticed because it seemed a little strange to him, one of the women appeared much younger than the other. He didn't say they were arguing."

"Interesting, interesting." Suzie pursed her lips. "I guess we should tell Jason about this." Before she could even pull out her phone Neil walked up to the front desk. He dropped his bag on the floor with a thump.

"I'm checking out."

"Neil, I'm very sorry…"

"I don't have time for this. Just do what you need to do to get me checked out of this place quickly."

Suzie nodded. She began filling out the last of the paperwork. "Neil, did Priscilla have any friends that were young women?"

"What?" He scowled at her. "I just want to check out."

"I was just wondering, if you knew of a young woman that she might associate with?" Suzie asked.

"The only friend she had was that damn bird, all right? Now, let's go." He tapped the desk.

"I just need your signature in these two places." Suzie pointed out the two spots on the paperwork. Neil signed the papers with two sharp strokes of his pen.

"There." He picked up his bag and strode

across the room and out the front door of Dune House. Suzie jumped at how hard he slammed the door.

"Wow, good riddance." Mary shook her head.

"Yes, well when he posts a scathing review on our website, we're going to care." Suzie sighed. "I'm sure there was a better way I could have handled that."

"Try not to worry about it. He might not even leave a review."

"Well, I will." Stewart smiled as he walked up to the desk. "I really enjoyed my stay here, ladies. I'm sorry that I have to cut it short."

"Stewart, I wish there was more we could have done to make you feel more comfortable," Mary said.

"To be honest with you, it's my guilt that is making me leave."

"Your guilt?" Mary leaned forward with interest. "Guilt about what?"

"Well, maybe if I had said something to Priscilla when I saw her, maybe if I had asked if she was okay. It was just that with the way she was limping, I figured she was drunk."

"Limping?" Suzie narrowed her eyes. "Wait a minute, when did you see Priscilla, Stewart?"

"Oh, the night she died. I saw her walking down the hall towards her room. I wish I would have asked if she was okay. Maybe if I offered to keep her company or something. Maybe she would still be alive if I had."

"It's not your fault, Stewart." Mary touched the back of his hand. "No one could have known what would happen."

"No Stewart, it's not your fault. But you may have been the last person to see Priscilla alive. I think it's important that you speak to Jason." Suzie picked up one of the business cards that she kept on the desk. "Please contact him and let him know what you saw."

"Oh wow, really? I didn't realize that." He

shook his head. "I'm sorry, Suzie, but like I said before, I don't want to get in the middle of a murder investigation."

"Stewart, you have to tell the police what you saw." Mary met his eyes.

"No. I don't. Now, please, I'd like to check out."

Suzie handed him the paper to sign. She was mystified as to why he wouldn't want to speak to the police about what he saw. She began to look at Stewart in a different way. He was withdrawn, hadn't spoken to Neil or Priscilla even once that she had seen, and had checked in the day before they arrived. Was it possible that he had been watching them the entire time? As he signed the paperwork he smiled.

"Please check for my glowing review, ladies. I will be back." He picked up his suitcase and walked towards the door. Suzie pulled out her cell phone and fired off a fast text to Jason about Stewart that warned him Stewart was about to leave town and he should be questioned before he did. Jason sent a text back that requested her presence at the police station. Suzie sighed.

"It looks like I'm going to have to go see Jason in person about this. Mary, since we don't have any more guests, do you want to join me?"

"Actually, I was thinking of walking into town and going to the library. You know how Louis knows the history of everyone in town and how good he is at researching people. I thought he might be able to find out who that woman is that was with Priscilla."

"Good plan. Are you sure you don't want a lift?" Suzie offered.

"No, I could use the fresh air."

"I'll tell you what, I'll meet you there after I talk to Jason. Okay?" Suzie said.

"Sure."

Suzie grabbed her purse and keys, but as she was about to walk out the door Mary stopped her with a travel mug of coffee and a muffin.

"It's important." She raised an eyebrow.

"Thank you, Mary."

Suzie hurried out the door to her car. She wondered why Jason wanted to see her in person. As she drove towards the police station she glanced at the clock on the dashboard. She hadn't yet heard from Paul that he had docked. That was a little odd, but she assumed that he must have been delayed for some reason. When she looked away from the clock she caught sight of the jewelry store, and a man who looked just like Paul was opening the door to it. Her heart skipped a beat. Paul was not the type of man to browse in a jewelry store. He also had not called to let her know that he was on dry land. She glanced in the rearview mirror, but the man was already gone.

"I must have been mistaken." She parked the car in the police station parking lot and walked inside. Jason and Kirk stood near Jason's desk. Suzie couldn't hear what they were saying, but their expressions were grave.

"Jason?" Suzie waited for him near the front desk. Jason waved her back.

"Did you see my text about Stewart?"

"Yes, I did. We have a big problem. I hope that the guys on patrol can catch him."

"Why is that?" Suzie looked past them at the computer screen. "Stewart has a record?"

"Yes. For assault. On an elderly woman." He scowled. "I can't believe I missed it. He was on my list of people I needed to question. I just hadn't caught up with him yet."

"He was so polite and quiet. I certainly didn't think that there was anything to be concerned about," Suzie said.

"What changed that?"

"Well, he told me that he saw Priscilla the night of the murder, going back to her room. I told him that he should contact you as he was likely one of the last people to see Priscilla alive. He refused. In fact he even checked out because there was an investigation. He must have known that he would be a prime suspect or he was concerned because he is the murderer."

"Are you sure he saw her that night? Maybe it was another night?"

"No. I don't think so. He said he thought she was drunk because she was limping."

"Like when she stumbled out of the restaurant," Jason said. "Yes, this is a good lead, I just wish we had caught him before he left."

"I'm sorry, I texted you as soon as I suspected."

"I appreciate that, Suzie."

"Oh, by the way Paul should be getting in today."

"I already talked to him." Jason looked back at the computer screen. "Suzie, I may need to ask you and Mary some more questions about Stewart."

"Uh huh." Suzie's mind reeled, not from Stewart being a suspect, but from Paul's arrival.

Why hadn't he called to tell her that he was back? Maybe that had been him at the jewelry shop. She gripped her phone for a moment. She thought about calling him, but she knew she would be heartbroken if he didn't answer. Maybe he wasn't as eager to see her as she was to see him. It hurt her to think it, but Suzie always did her best to come to the logical conclusion. There must be a good reason why Paul would go out of his way to contact Jason, but not even bother to text her.

Chapter Nine

Suzie was still trying to think of a reason why Paul wouldn't call her when she left the police station and drove to the library. She sat in her car for a few minutes while she waited for her emotions to settle. Every minute that slipped by without Paul calling her made her sink deeper into confusion. She tried to figure out if she'd done or said anything to upset him. As she recalled when they said goodbye before he left on his trip everything was just fine. Short of a mermaid she couldn't imagine who he could have met while out on the water.

Suzie shook her head and tried to focus her attention on the case. Although Jason appeared to be convinced that he had his man, Suzie was not so sure. Why would Stewart stay for as long as he had if he was involved? Why had he been so kind? Perhaps to throw them off?

Suzie opened the car door and stepped out.

The library was not very crowded as it was still early in the day. When she stepped inside she saw Louis and Mary hunched together around one of the computers. With a bright smile on her lips she walked up to them.

"Morning."

"Morning." Louis peered through his thick glasses at her.

"Were you able to find anything?" Suzie maintained her smile.

"Louis is amazing." Mary patted his shoulder. "He did an image search on Priscilla to see if he could find any pictures of her with a young woman. He did."

"Yes, I did. Ladies, let me introduce Leanne Kay, formerly known as Leanne Kane, until she changed her name on her eighteenth birthday."

Suzie leaned over Louis' shoulder and peered at the computer screen. An image of Priscilla accompanied by a tall, young woman with a blonde ponytail popped up on the screen.

"She has a daughter?"

"Yes. Not just any daughter. She has a hardcore modern day hippie daughter."

"Flowerchild?" Mary raised an eyebrow.

"Not these days. They're called tree huggers nowadays. There's a large global environmentalist movement and it grows every day. Priscilla's daughter is a rising star in the movement. She's been to several high-risk environments for the purpose of rescuing endangered species from war-torn areas or global developments."

"So Priscilla, who's all about profit not about protecting the environment, has a daughter that wants to save the world," Mary said.

"I imagine that they didn't get along very well, I mean her daughter changed her last name." Louis tapped the screen. "I found one article where Priscilla is questioned about her daughter and she has a pretty powerful response. And I quote, 'I raised her, provided her with all that she needed, and now she is her own person. I wouldn't expect anything less from her.' So basically stating they have nothing to do with each other."

"Or that she's proud of her independent-minded daughter." Mary crossed her arms. "I find it hard to believe that Priscilla was as detached as she claimed."

"Not everyone is as loving a mother as you, Mary." Suzie sighed. "Maybe Priscilla wasn't the mothering type."

"Maybe." Mary narrowed her eyes. "But the way she doted on that bird tells me that she is quite nurturing. That is the mothering type."

"Good point," Suzie agreed. "I didn't think about that. What about the father?"

"Actually, there's no father that I can find. It looks like Leanne was the product of a single mother by choice."

"What do you mean?" Mary furrowed her brow.

"He means that Priscilla hit up a sperm bank

when she was ready to be a mommy."

Mary's eyes widened. "I wish I had thought of that."

"Mary!" Suzie laughed.

"It would have saved me some trouble." Mary smirked.

"Oh, look at this." Louis smiled. "I think I just won the lottery."

"What is it?" Suzie looked back at the computer.

"It looks like Leanne was, and may still be in town. She came here to defend the seabirds that may be affected by her mother's vast development. Apparently, they nest along Redhawk River and since it's so close to the construction zone, they will be impacted."

"That must have been who she argued with at the restaurant! Of course. Only a mother and daughter can fight like that."

"So, if she was at dinner with her mother last

night, then she is probably staying here in town. The funny thing is, I don't recall seeing her at the community meeting. Do you, Mary?" Suzie asked.

"No, but it did get pretty chaotic. Maybe we just didn't notice her?"

"I don't think Leanne is the type to be seen and not heard." Louis clicked the print button and the printer sprang to life. "I'll give you a copy of her photograph so you can keep an eye out for her."

"I can give it to Jason." Suzie took the paper from the printer. "Thanks."

"Are you sure you want to tell Jason right away? Maybe we should see if we can find her first," Mary suggested.

"Why?" Suzie met her eyes. "Is something wrong, Mary?"

"If Leanne didn't kill her mother, then she may not even know that her mother is dead, yet. I'd hate for her first introduction to that news to be a pair of handcuffs."

"Subtlety is not Jason's strong suit." Suzie pulled out her phone. "It will make his job easier if we track her down first anyway."

"If she killed her mother she probably hopped the first plane out of town," Mary said.

"Maybe." Suzie tilted her head back and forth. "And maybe not." She waited for someone to pick up the line.

"Hello?"

"Hi Maurice, I have a question for you."

"Suzie? Suzie Allen?"

"Yes."

"How dare you call me!"

"I'm sorry?"

"Your cousin was here accusing me of murder. How do you like that?"

"I had to tell him that you were at Dune House, but I certainly didn't tell him that you were a murderer."

"Oh no? That's funny, because while he was

here he certainly seemed convinced of my guilt, all because of you."

"I'm sorry I don't mean to correct you, Maurice, but I think that was much more because of you. After all you decided to sneak around Dune House. You almost started a riot at the community meeting. You gave Jason all the reason to suspect you. I didn't do any of that."

"Sure, I'll remember to ask you the next time I need someone to throw me under a bus, since you already have so much experience at it."

Suzie rolled her eyes. "Maurice, stop! If you're so worried about being arrested then you should be happy to help me. Can you please tell me if Leanne Kay stayed at your motel or is currently staying there?"

"I don't want to help you with anything."

"Don't you hang up, Maurice. You're the prime suspect. You say that you didn't kill Priscilla, I believe you. But that means we need a new suspect. So answer the question."

"All right fine. Yes, she is staying here. Checked in three days ago."

"Is she still there now?"

"I don't know if she's in her room or not, but she hasn't checked out."

"Great. If she tries to check out, stall her."

"Stall her?"

"Yes Maurice, chat, try to have a friendly conversation, you know?"

"I don't know. I don't want any part in this."

"You're already in it, Maurice. Please, just stall her."

"All right, all right." He groaned. "How soon can you be here?"

"About ten minutes."

"I'll do what I can, but I'm not making any promises, Suzie."

"Thanks, Maurice." Suzie hung up the phone.

"What are you planning, Suzie?" Mary looked

over at her.

"I'm just going to see if I can speak to Leanne. See what she knows and try to work out if she was involved in this."

"Do you want me to come with you?"

"I think that might be a good idea. You're much more sensitive to these things than I am."

"Thanks for your help, Louis." Mary smiled at him. "You did good."

"I do what I can." Louis grinned. "Just do me a favor and let me know how it all turns out."

As Suzie and Mary left the library, Suzie frowned. "I think that Jason is going to be pretty upset if he finds out we kept this from him, so we better make this fast."

"I think it's the right thing to do. Leanne may be a suspect in Jason's eyes, but to me, she's a daughter, who might not even know her mother is dead, let alone that she was murdered," Mary said. "Come, let's go. You might hear from Paul soon and then you'll have other things to do."

Mary grinned. Suzie's smile faded. She glanced away from Mary.

"You may be right about that."

"Suzie?" Mary grabbed her arm gently. "What's wrong?"

"Huh? Nothing is wrong." Suzie shrugged. "We'd better hurry."

"No way, don't you take one step until you tell me what is going on." Mary crossed her arms.

"Mary, I said nothing is wrong."

"And I know you're lying to me, which you never do, so it must be something very serious. What's going on, Suzie? Tell me."

"It's nothing really. It's just that Paul is already here, and he hasn't called to tell me."

"Then how do you know he's here?"

"Jason told me he already spoke to him. Also, I saw him at a jewelry shop early this morning."

"A jewelry shop?" Mary clapped her hands. "Do you know what this means?"

"Should I?" Suzie narrowed her eyes. "I don't know. Maybe he's lost interest?"

"No Suzie!" Mary laughed. "He's being sneaky, he's at a jewelry shop, come on, put two and two together."

"I don't follow." Suzie sighed.

"He's going to propose, Suzie!" Mary clapped again. "He was probably at the jewelry shop to buy you a ring."

"What? That's nonsense. We haven't even been dating that long, and that's ridiculous. We're too old to get married."

"Too old?" Mary shook her head. "There's no age limit to love, darling."

"Mary, stop it. That's crazy. Why would he even think that's a good idea?"

"Maybe because he loves you?" Mary searched her eyes. "Would it really be so bad?"

"For me? Yes. I have no interest in getting married. What then? Would we live together?"

She scrunched up her nose. "Could you imagine?"

"Uh yes. I think about living with Wes all the time."

"Oh, no you're not..."

"No, we're not. But I do think about it. I rather miss having someone to snuggle up to and wake up next to."

"I'm not much for sharing my room." Suzie shook her head. "No, no, that would be a disaster."

"Aw." Mary hugged her. "Well, maybe I'm wrong. You never know. If he does propose though, make sure you let him down easy, Suzie. A man's heart gets broken very easily, and once it is, it's hard to fix."

Suzie frowned. "We'd better get to the motel before we miss our chance to talk to Leanne."

"You're right." Mary sighed. "I'm sorry that I didn't make you feel better, Suzie."

"It's all right. I just hope that you're wrong. I think I'd rather find out he's dating someone else."

Mary held her gaze. "No you wouldn't, Suzie. That I don't believe for a second."

Suzie offered her a half smile and nodded. "You're right."

Chapter Ten

As Suzie drove with Mary towards the motel she thought about what Mary had said. She sorted through her memories in an attempt to remember whether she had ever spoken to Paul about marriage. He seemed to be as content as she was with the way things were. She couldn't imagine what it would be like to have someone live with her, in her room. To take turns for the shower.

"Ugh, no thanks," Suzie said under her breath and shuddered. She pulled into the parking lot of the motel. Maurice stood outside near the front door of the office, but there was no sign of Leanne. Suzie and Mary got out of the car and walked towards Maurice. Maurice glared at Suzie as she approached.

"Where is she?" Suzie glanced at the row of doors that led to the motel rooms.

"As far as I know she's still in there. Room three. That's as much as I'm getting involved.

Understand?"

"Perfectly." Suzie glanced over at Mary. Mary grimaced. The two walked towards room three. Suzie knocked on the door. After a moment, the door opened. Before them stood the person who was in the photograph that Louis had printed.

"Leanne Kay?" Suzie met her eyes. They were hooded with dark circles underneath.

"Yes. What is it?" She wiped at her eyes. "I'm not doing any press."

"We're not the press." Mary's voice was gentle as she spoke. "May we come inside?"

"Why?" Leanne narrowed her eyes. "What is this about?"

"It's about your mother, Priscilla."

"What about her?" Leanne stood straight up. Suzie and Mary exchanged a quick glance. "She's passed away."

Suzie and Mary relaxed slightly as they felt a sense of relief that they wouldn't have to be the ones to break the bad news to her.

"We're sorry for your loss," Mary said sympathetically.

"Thank you. I just don't know why it happened, now." Leanne wiped at her eyes. "She and I just fixed things."

"Fixed things, how?" Suzie raised an eyebrow.

"She finally saw things from my point of view. I took her to see the nests. I took her to Redhawk River."

Suzie's stomach lurched. Had Leanne just revealed where Priscilla was murdered?

"Did you and your mother have a disagreement while you were at the river?" Suzie asked.

"No. My mother and I fought at dinner, but after dinner I showed her the reality. I showed her the nests and how much damage would be done. You know she loves that bird she has. I guess I finally got through to her when she realized that she would be hurting birds. She was going to call off the deal. She promised me that she would."

"When was the last time that you saw your mother, Leanne?" Suzie asked.

"It was that night. It was the last time I saw her. But I called her driver to drop her off at the bed and breakfast where she was staying. She broke her heel, and I was afraid if she walked she might get hurt. So, I called her driver. I don't even know if she made it home."

Suzie's eyes narrowed. Conner hadn't mentioned anything about picking up Priscilla. She began to think that maybe Leanne was telling the truth. Suzie reached into her purse and pulled out Jason's card.

"Have you spoken to the police?" Suzie asked.

"No why?"

"You need to contact him right away," Suzie said as she handed the card to Leanne. "He's investigating the murder..."

"Murder?" Leanne gulped and her eyes widened. "She was murdered?"

"Yes, Leanne, I'm so sorry." Mary gave her a hug. "I know this is a lot to take in. But anything you can tell Jason might help."

"Okay. Okay." She nodded. "I'll call him right now." She went back into the motel room and retrieved her cell phone.

Mary tugged Suzie aside.

"We need to be careful what we say," Mary said. "She looks so upset."

"People can fake it. She certainly had motive to kill her mother. And means and opportunity," Suzie said.

"Do you really think that she did it?"

"I think that there's one good way to find out. I'm going to go to Redhawk River and get a sample of the water. If Summer can match it, then we will at least know where Priscilla was killed."

"I'm going to stay with her until Jason gets here. I don't think she should be alone."

"That's good. I'll let you know what I find at

the river. Call me if you need a lift."

"I will but I'm sure I'll be fine, I can walk."

"Okay, I won't be long."

"Suzie, be careful." Mary squeezed her hand.

"I will be."

Suzie climbed into her car. Just as she was about to start it, her cell phone rang. Her heart stopped when she saw that it was Paul. For a moment she considered ignoring it. Before it could go to voicemail she grabbed it up.

"Hello?"

"Hi beautiful."

She smiled, despite her concerns. She loved the way he greeted her. "Hi handsome."

"I just got in, I heard about what happened. Are you doing okay?"

"I think so."

"Can we meet for a bite?"

"I'm on my way to go for a hike."

"A hike?"

"Yes, near Redhawk River."

There was a long pause. Suzie bit into her bottom lip. She wondered what he was thinking.

"I've been looking forward to seeing you."

"I'm sorry, Paul. We can meet up later."

"Maybe I could join you for the hike?"

Suzie grimaced. She knew that he was lying to her about just getting in. Why would he do that unless he was hiding something?

"Of course you can. I would love that. But you're not too tired?" Even though she suspected he was up to something she still wanted to see him.

"I'm never too tired to spend time with you, Suzie."

"Aw. I'll be there in five minutes."

"That's what I call service."

Suzie laughed as she hung up the phone. Despite the stress of the murder, Paul always found a way to make her laugh. She changed direction and drove towards the dock. As she approached it she thought about how lucky she was to have found him. It was an unexpected relationship, but one that she was very happy with. She just hoped he wasn't going to do anything that would change that.

Chapter Eleven

When Suzie pulled up to the docks she noticed that there were not very many people milling about. Suzie thought about the resort taking over part of the coastline of Garber. It wasn't until that moment that she truly understood why everyone was so upset about the possibility. The quiet piece of paradise was all theirs for the time being, the moment that it became a resort town, it would no longer be a hidden gem for mainly the local residents to enjoy. She was lost in thought when Paul opened the passenger side door of the car. The sudden movement and sound caused every muscle in her body to jerk.

"Oh Suzie, I'm sorry if I startled you. I thought you saw me."

"It's okay." Suzie laughed. "I guess I was just distracted."

Paul leaned across the car to hug her. His

familiar scent and warmth surrounded her. "I missed you."

"I missed you too, Paul." Suzie lingered in his arms for a moment, then she pulled away. "Was it a good trip?"

"It wasn't bad." He shrugged. "It could have been better. I'm sorry about what happened to Priscilla. It's hard to believe that someone could be so cruel."

"It's even harder to believe that it might have been her own daughter, Leanne that did it."

"Her daughter?" Paul gasped.

"That's why I'm going to the river. If I can prove that the water in Priscilla's lungs is the same water that runs in the river then I think Jason will be able to make an arrest."

"I can't say it surprises me that you're involved in all of this. Thanks for letting me tag along."

Suzie shot him a smile as she started the car. She drove towards the river based on the directions that the GPS provided. It took her down several windy, tree-lined roads. When they arrived at a small dirt parking lot she stopped the car. Paul hopped out and walked around to meet her at the other side of the car. The two embraced again and shared a small kiss.

"I'm so glad to be home." He smiled as he looked into her eyes. Suzie smiled in return but broke the visual connection before it could linger.

"I just need to get a small sample of the water."

"Are you sure this is the right place?" Paul looked at the thick underbrush. "It doesn't look like anyone has been here for a long time."

"I know that Leanne and Priscilla were here together the night that Priscilla was killed. Leanne claims that her mother changed her mind about the development deal, but I find that hard to believe."

"Maybe she came to her senses." Paul pulled back some branches so that Suzie could step through. "I'd rather think that, than anything else."

"Me too. But the water will reveal the truth. Someone drowned Priscilla and then dumped her body in or near the ocean."

"If they drowned her here then why would that person move the body to another location?"

"In an attempt to make it look like an accident. I guess whoever did this thought that people would just assume, as the police first did, that it was an accidental drowning. Without an investigation into the death, they would have gotten away with it."

The foliage was dense around the edge of the river. Suzie held on to Paul's hand as they made their way through it.

"Do you really think this will help the investigation? It will be enough for Jason to make an arrest?"

"I don't think that it can hurt it. Summer said that if she had a sample to compare the water to then she might be able to pinpoint the crime scene. If the water matches then I think we can be fairly certain Leanne killed her mother. At the very least the crime scene investigators can search the area for any evidence."

Paul shoved his hands deep down into the pockets of his thick jeans and looked out over the area. Suzie pushed some reeds aside from the water's edge. She dipped the small container into the water and collected a sample. When she stood back up Paul grasped her arm to keep her steady.

"This should do it." Suzie sealed the vial then dropped it into her purse.

"We're already out here we might as well enjoy a little stroll." Paul tipped his head towards a trail that led away from the river. Suzie eyed him for a moment. She had heard plenty of proposal stories over the years and most involved a beautiful setting, such as the woods they were in.

"Oh, I don't know. I really need to get this sample back to the lab."

"A few minutes?" He stroked the back of her hand. "I'd love just a little time alone with you." Suzie tried to think of any excuse to prevent a walk through the woods, but from the way Paul's eyes squinted, she knew he would see right through any ploy.

"Okay sure. A short one."

As they walked hand in hand along the trail Suzie glanced over at him. His expression was as casual as always. Nothing about it indicated that he kept a secret. But Suzie was certain that he was.

"How was the weather on the water?"

"It was nice. Not a single squall."

"I'm glad. You got back a bit late." Suzie left the opening there for him. She wanted him to admit that he docked earlier than he claimed.

"Hm." Paul shrugged. He paused beside a very large flowering tree. "Isn't this gorgeous?" Suzie looked up at the tree.

"Yes, it is quite beautiful." When she looked back at Paul he was down on one knee.

140

"Oh no, Paul. No!" Suzie stumbled back a step. Paul glanced over at her.

"What's wrong?"

"This isn't the right time and..."

"Huh?" He tugged the laces on his shoe and tied them tightly. "It's not the right time for what?" He stood up. Suzie flushed as she looked away from him.

"I'm sorry, I don't know what I was thinking."

"Hey, it's okay. You've been through a lot of stress lately." He locked his eyes to hers. "I'm a little worried about you. I know that your instincts are good and you can solve any problem, but maybe this one is a little too intense for you."

"No. I'm fine, really. I was just confused."

"Not about me I hope."

"No, not at all."

"Okay good." He took her hand again.

Suzie smiled, but the heat in her cheeks did not fade. "I should really get this sample to

Summer. I don't want it to sit too long."

"Okay. Let's head back." He slid his arm around her waist. Her skin prickled with a familiar warmth in reaction to his touch, but her rapid heart rate remained. "Suzie?" He met her eyes. "Is something wrong?"

"I'm just a little shaken up by all of this." Suzie glanced away.

"I don't believe that for a second."

"What?" Suzie looked back at him.

"I've seen you shaken up, and this is not that. What's going on?"

Suzie smiled a little. Paul did know her better than she expected. "I'm just a little uneasy I guess."

"All right, if you don't want to talk about it that's fine. Have dinner with me tonight? On the boat?"

"Oh, I don't know."

"Please." He smiled.

"With all that's going on it might not be a good idea."

"All that's going on is exactly the reason that you need a break. I'm sure that there's one hour of the day that you can spare. Hmm?" His jaw set and his shoulders squared. Suzie was quite familiar with the stance he took. It declared that he was going to be stubborn.

"Yes." Suzie leaned into his shoulder. "For you, definitely."

"Great. Now let's get that sample back to Summer. The sooner you get to the bottom of all of this the sooner this town can go back to normal."

Chapter Twelve

Suzie dropped Paul off back at the dock before she continued on to the medical examiner's office. When she stepped inside she heard Summer's music playing.

"Hello?"

"Hold on, Suzie, I'll be right out." The music turned off. Summer walked out of the back room to greet her. "What's up?"

"I have a sample from Redhawk River. I think it's the area where Priscilla might have been killed." Suzie held out the vial.

"Oh wow, great! Thank you, Suzie." Summer took the vial. "I will get this tested right away. If it is a match then I'll obviously have to get a sample tested that was collected through the official channels, but we can start with this. We really need to find the crime scene. I think that will make all the difference in the case. I've never seen Jason so frustrated. He has plenty of suspects, but nothing solid to go on. So, hopefully this will help."

"I didn't realize this was getting to him so much."

"Something sure is. He's been jittery and distracted. I tried to get him to have lunch with me and he turned me down. I think it's the first time he ever has."

"Well, there's a lot of pressure around this case and a lot of attention. Jason's probably in a hurry to get it over with, just like we all are."

"To be honest with you, Suzie, I'm in no hurry. In my line of work a slow, steady pace and precision is key. If I make one mistake, it can mean that Priscilla never gets her justice. That's why I evaluate everything about the body."

"You do a very good job, Summer. Will you let me know when you get the results of the water test?"

"Absolutely. Thanks for going to so much trouble. What made you think that the river might be the place?"

"I spoke with Priscilla's daughter, Leanne, and she said that she and her mother went out to the river together the night she died."

"I see." Summer frowned. "I'll let you know."

"Thanks." Suzie left the office and drove towards Dune House. When she parked she noticed that Wes' car was there as well. She walked into the lobby to find Wes and Mary cooing at the bird.

"What are you two doing?" Suzie tried not to laugh.

Mary grinned. "We're trying to get this bird to say anything other than pumpkin."

"Good luck." Suzie shook her head. "I haven't heard it say anything else since Priscilla's death."

"It's not unusual for a bird to parrot a word they hear frequently," Mary said. "Pumpkin is just a rather odd word for it to hear often enough to retain."

"That's true." Suzie laughed. "I think I've said it more since the bird has arrived than I have in a lifetime."

"Oh, by the way I ran into Jason in town and he had just finished questioning Leanne." Wes straightened up and turned to look at Suzie. "I thought that you might want to know what he found out from Leanne."

"Sure, what did he tell you?" Suzie asked.

"She told him the same thing she told you and Mary, that she and her mother had gone out to Redhawk River. But he pushed for more information. I guess she and her mother had been in contact quite a bit. He found proof of it in their phone records. Leanne and Priscilla spoke on a daily basis for at least a month before Priscilla arrived here," Wes explained.

"That's odd, isn't it? I thought they were estranged?" Suzie glanced towards Mary, who nodded.

"They were. I guess that Leanne admitted that

she and her mother were not exactly talking. They were arguing," Wes said. "Each and every call Leanne attempted to get her mother to agree to back out of the deal. But Priscilla would insist that she already made a commitment to her business partner and there was no way for her to change her mind."

"That must have been quite frustrating for Leanne." Suzie narrowed her eyes. "All of that resentment must have built up."

"It also makes it seem impossible that Priscilla would suddenly change her mind about the deal. If after all of the arguing she still resisted, then why would one walk through the woods change anything?"

"Exactly." Suzie sighed. "It looks like Leanne might just be the murderer. I took a sample of water from the river to Summer. Once she confirms that it matches the water in Priscilla's lungs then we'll be able to settle all of this."

"Jason tried to hold her with what he had, but

he didn't have enough. He had to let her go." Wes sighed. "That's one of the worst parts of police work, knowing who the criminal is, and not being able to do anything about it."

"What if she takes off?" Suzie shook her head. "She has no reason not to run if she thinks that she is a suspect. How could they just let her walk out?"

"His hands are tied, Suzie. It's not Jason's fault," Wes said.

"Well, then we need to get some real evidence. There's no time to wait for the water report to come back."

"What do you mean, Suzie?" Mary studied her. Suzie met Mary's eyes and then glanced over at Wes.

"I think it's something that we need to discuss in private, Mary."

"Anything you can say to Mary in private I'm sure you can say in front of me." Wes folded his arms across his chest. "Unless of course you intend to get her into some kind of illegal activities. Is that the case?"

Suzie raised an eyebrow. "What happens between Mary and me stays between Mary and me."

"Is that so?" His laughter had an impatient edge.

"Yes, it is so." Mary placed a hand on Wes' shoulder. "There's a lot of things that Suzie and I can only tell each other. That's non-negotiable."

"So is Suzie putting you in any kind of danger!" Wes' eyes narrowed. "You have to be careful."

"I would never do anything to put Mary at risk, Wes. If you don't know that, then you and I need to spend a lot more time together."

"All right, all right." He held up his hands. "In my experience when the two of you get together some very interesting things happen."

"But we're both still here, right?" Mary smiled. "I appreciate your desire to protect me,

Wes, but I've made it through many decades and the only person who has had my back through every single moment of that time, is Suzie. We take care of each other. So, you may worry if you wish, but it will be a waste of your time."

"Please excuse me for attempting to get in the middle of something so sacred. You're right. I may have overstepped. I'm sorry, Suzie."

"Don't be." Suzie smiled. "Anyone who cares about Mary enough to want to ensure her safety, even from me, is someone I respect."

"That's gracious of you, Suzie." Wes winked at her. "I'll be on the porch if either of you need me."

Even with Wes out on the porch Suzie pulled Mary into the kitchen to talk. "Thanks for coming to my defense."

"Wes means well, he's just always in detective mode."

"His instincts aren't wrong. I do want to get you involved in something illegal and potentially dangerous."

"Well, why else would we need to talk in private?" Mary grinned. "What is it?"

"Neil managed to check out of his room before it was ever searched. I don't want the same thing to happen with Leanne. Jason can't go in without a warrant, but I think there has to be some kind of proof in there. I think we should break in."

"What if we are caught?" Mary frowned.

"We just have to make sure we aren't. I want the chance to see what Leanne might be hiding before it's too late."

"I think it's a good idea," Mary paused and peeked out of the kitchen. "We'll have to get rid of Wes first."

"We have to go soon because I have dinner with Paul tonight."

"Well, we can't have you miss that." Mary winked. "Let me send him on his way, then we can head out."

"Wait, we need to make sure that Leanne is not in her room, too." Suzie considered her options for a moment. "I know what to do. Go ahead and deal with Wes."

As soon as Mary left the kitchen, Suzie placed a call to Louis. "I know, I know, it's me again."

"I don't mind. What can I do for you, Suzie?"

"Is there any way that you could send an anonymous message to someone?"

"Several ways."

"I want to get Leanne out of her motel room. The only way I can be sure to do that is if there is a problem at Redhawk River."

"Oh, maybe a fire?"

"That would probably work, but I wouldn't want to alarm anyone else or get the fire department involved."

"Hm. Maybe something more personal then. I know. Why don't I send her a message that there's going to be a rally for the seabirds in town. By the time she figures out that it's not happening you should have enough time to go through her room."

"Perfect. Thanks Louis. Let's hope it works."

"No need to hope when I'm on the case, you can be certain."

Suzie smiled at his confidence. She met Mary on the porch just as Wes pulled out of the parking lot.

"He wasn't upset I hope?"

"No, he was fine. I told him we needed some girl time, and he had no problem with fleeing." Mary laughed. "Sometimes I wonder what men think women do during girl time."

"Well, apparently we stage break-ins and solve murders." Suzie grinned. "Let's head straight for the motel. Louis is setting some bait to draw Leanne out, but we won't know if it worked until we get there."

"This isn't your way of avoiding dinner with Paul is it?"

"Not at all." Suzie glanced at her watch. "We'd

better hurry if we're going to get back in plenty of time for me to gussy up for Paul."

"Gussy up? Really?"

Suzie grinned.

Chapter Thirteen

On the drive to the motel Suzie peppered Mary with the details of Louis' plan.

"That should work. But we don't know for how long. We will have to move as fast as possible," Mary said.

"Yes, and we have to watch out for Maurice, too." Mary started to pull into the parking lot of the motel, but Suzie gestured for her to keep driving. "Let's park in the next plaza. That way Maurice won't notice the car."

"Good idea." Mary parked the car. The two walked towards the motel behind the shops in the plaza and crossed onto the motel property behind the building. Suzie counted the windows to figure out which room belonged to Leanne. The parking lot was fairly empty. Perhaps the news of the murder had scared some people off, or the majority of Maurice's guests were out enjoying the day. Either way it worked to their benefit.

Suzie noticed that Maurice's car appeared to be missing as well.

"I'm going to take a look in the window to see if she's in there."

"I'll walk around to the front and knock." Mary headed for the front of the building. Suzie peered through the back window of the motel room. The flimsy curtain did nothing to hide the interior of the room. From what she could tell Leanne was not in the room. She gave Mary some time to knock. There was no movement in the room.

Suzie tried to open the window. As she hoped it would be, it was unlocked. She eased the window open and hoisted one leg over. In her mind she lithely climbed into the room. In reality her foot caught on the corner of the curtain and she fell forward flat onto her stomach on the bed. As fast as she could she got to her feet. One quick glance around informed her that there was no one else in the room with her. She grabbed the corner of the bedspread and looked under the bed. When

157

she straightened up she heard a scuffle at the window. A sharp breath caught in her chest as she spun around to find Mary with one foot over the windowsill.

"Mary, what are you doing?"

"I'm trying to get in the window."

"No! Just stay out there and be a lookout."

"Oh, you get to have all of the fun." Mary huffed and crossed her arms. Suzie smiled and began picking her way through the small motel room. It was drab in comparison to the rooms she was used to at Dune House. She noticed Leanne's suitcase which stuck out of the closet. When she flipped it open all she found inside were a few t-shirts and pants. She poked her head in the bathroom and spotted a toothbrush and a small hairbrush. There was nothing so far to implicate Leanne in a crime. She discovered a well-read book left on the bed. Other than that there weren't many personal items. Then Suzie spotted it, a datebook on the bedside table. She picked it up and began to flip through it. Many of the pages were filled with contacts and appointments. However, in the notes section it appeared to be more like a diary. She began to read through some of it.

How I could have sprung from the womb of a woman so callous, so ignorant, is beyond me. I long for the day when I am able to make her face the consequences of all the damage that her power and money have caused.

Another entry was just as infuriated.

Once more the devil I call mother will destroy what I hold most dear. It's not enough that she abandoned me as a child in the pursuit of money, now she will make mother birds abandon their nests and eggs, all to ensure a little more profit. If there is ever anything I can do to stop her, I must do it. I can't be faint of heart. I can't be intimidated by her goon, Runkin. I must be brave enough to put a stop to all of this.

Suzie's heart skipped a beat. She knew that there was no way that she could give the datebook to Jason to use as evidence as she had broken in to see it. But there was no question in her mind that Leanne hated Priscilla more than enough to harm her. However, there was one other thing that stood out to her in the notes, her hatred for Neil Runkin as well.

"Suzie? I heard a car pull into the parking lot."

"Okay, I'm done here anyway." Suzie made a smoother exit than entrance. Once on the other side she eased the window closed. Carefully they made their way back across the parking lot and into the next plaza. Suzie's heart still raced even when they reached their car.

"What did you find?" Mary fumbled with the keys to get the lock on the door open.

"I found something rather interesting. I'm

going to put in a call to Louis and see if he can help me with something. I could do it myself, but I think Louis will be quicker and probably more successful. It seems that Leanne had a particular dislike for Priscilla's business partner, Neil. Her diary is full of hatred towards her mother as well. Several times she states that she will do anything to stop her mother from causing more harm to the environment."

"Wow, that certainly makes her feelings quite clear."

"I also don't think it's possible that the two made up as easily as Leanne claims. I'm going to make a quick call to Louis, and then I have to get back to Dune House and get ready for my dinner with Paul."

"Do you think tonight will be the night?" Mary winked at her.

"I hope not." Suzie sighed. "Do you think a man has ever stayed with a woman if she turned his proposal down?"

"You're really not interested, are you?"

"I love Paul." Suzie stared down at her own reflection in the screen of her phone. "I feel for him in ways that I've never felt for anyone. But that doesn't change the fact that I like things exactly as they are. I don't want to give up what we have right now."

"You wouldn't really have to give it up."

"Sure I would. Marriage would become a big priority for me. I love being with Paul, I just love having my own space as well. What we have works, why change it. Is love any less strong without a piece of paper?"

"I understand what you're saying, Suzie. To be honest with you, Paul might be a little hurt if you turn him down, but if he loves you the way I know he does, then he will get over it. It should matter to him more that you are content with what you have, than any piece of paper. If that's not the case, well then he might not be the right person for you."

"I agree. But I hate to think that. I do enjoy his company. I care for him more than I ever expected to."

"Yes, it does take you by surprise." Mary shook her head. "After what happened with my ex, I never imagined I'd want to be close to anyone again. But now I can't imagine my life without Wes. It is quite strange how things can change so fast."

"You're right about that." Suzie nodded. "Let's go, you drive and I can make the call on our way." Once they were on the road Suzie dialed Louis' cell phone number.

"Hi Suzie."

"Hi Louis. Are you busy right now?"

"Not really. It's been a slow day."

"Would you mind checking into something for me?"

"Sure. What is it?"

"Can you see if you can find out if Leanne Kay

163

and Neil Runkin had any run-ins, confrontations?"

"If someone took a picture of it or wrote an article about it, I might be able to find it. Give me an hour and I'll see what I can dig up."

"Thanks Louis, you're the best."

"Yes, yes I am." He laughed as he hung up the phone.

"Do you think he'll be able to find something?" Mary looked over at her.

"Yes, I hope so. In the meantime there's not much that the datebook can provide Jason with and I can't really let him know that I've seen it as then I'd have to explain that I broke in," Suzie said as they pulled into the parking lot of Dune House.

"That won't go down well."

Suzie went straight up to her room to get ready to meet Paul. She sorted through her clothes to find something to wear, but it was hard for her to concentrate. Finally, she decided on a blouse and jeans. She didn't want to look as if she was trying too hard, but she also didn't want to look too casual. Once she was dressed Suzie walked into the living room to find Mary curled up on the couch with a blanket and a book.

"No Wes tonight?"

"Not tonight." Mary held up her book. "I have a different kind of date. Have fun tonight!"

"I will, I hope." Suzie grinned.

"Don't let what I said get to you, Suzie. You know Paul better than I do. If you two haven't even discussed the subject then I'm probably wrong about the proposal."

"That is a good point, Mary. Maybe I am worrying too much about it. Paul's not one to rush into things."

"See?" Mary smiled. "Now, just go and enjoy yourself."

"Thanks Mary. I will." She leaned down and gave her friend a warm hug.

When she drove away from Dune House she

did her best to keep her mind focused on the moment rather than what might happen in the future.

Chapter Fourteen

Suzie parked at the dock just as twilight thickened. The last of the evening light lingered on the glassy surface of the water. She paused to soak in the beauty for a moment. Everything about Garber was beautiful. She barely recalled her condo in the city anymore. She had adjusted very well to small town life. She walked along the dock to Paul's boat. When she stepped onto the deck the boat rocked just enough to make her grip the railing. The door to the interior of the boat swung open.

"There you are." Paul smiled. "I just started to wonder if you might be standing me up."

"Paul, I would never do that." Suzie placed a light kiss on his cheek.

"I hope not." He wrapped his arms around her and looked into her eyes. "Do you know how much I think of you when I'm out on the water?"

"How much?" Suzie grinned. A faint blush

colored Paul's weathered cheeks.

"Let's just say you're officially a distraction."

"Oh dear, I'm not sure if that's a good thing or a bad thing."

"It's a very, very, good thing." Paul smiled. "Come on in." Paul stepped back from the door. Suzie smiled at the candle that flickered on the small table in the middle of the living space. It wasn't a large area, but Paul made it work. "I wanted to put the table on the deck, but there's a chance of rain. I thought it would be better if we were inside tonight. I hope that you don't mind."

"This is perfect, Paul. Thank you so much, but you didn't have to go to all of this trouble. Cheeseburgers would have been just fine."

"Did you just mention cheeseburgers to a fisherman?" He raised an eyebrow.

"Oops." Suzie grinned.

He led her further into the boat. Suzie had added a few touches to the interior to make it a bit more livable. Soft cushions lined the benches and

168

Paul's bed had a brand new bedding set. "Of course it's fish." He gestured to the table.

"Lovely. I've been looking forward to dining on something you caught." As they sat down at the table Suzie watched him with a nervous smile. "I have to say this is a very nice bright spot in the middle of all the madness I've been dealing with."

"I imagine it might be hard for you to relax with everything on your mind." He poured two glasses of wine, then handed her one.

"Ah yes, thank you, this should help." She took a sip. "Delicious."

"It is, isn't it?" Paul said.

Suzie picked up her fork and began to eat some of the fish. "Oh wow, Paul, this is amazing."

"Is it?" He took a bite as well. "Yes, it is."

They sat in silence while they enjoyed their meal.

Suzie reached for her glass, but her hand moved a bit too fast. She knocked into the glass and splashed wine all over her white blouse. "Oh no! I'm such a klutz." She frowned. Paul jumped up and handed her a napkin.

"You're not a klutz. The boat might have rocked a bit. I'm so used to it that I don't even notice."

"Excuse me for just a moment, Paul. I want to see if I can rinse this a bit."

"There are some clean shirts in the drawer if you want to put something else on, Suzie. You can change in my room."

"Thank you." She ducked into the small bedroom and slid the door closed behind her. One look at the wine stain on her blouse made it clear that there was little hope for it. She sighed and opened one of the drawers in Paul's dresser. She reached in and pulled out one of Paul's t-shirts. When she did a black velvet box flipped out of the t-shirt. It landed in the drawer. The moment that Suzie saw it her heart stopped. It began to pound again only when she picked the box up. "It can't be. It's not what I think. It must be earrings or a necklace." She couldn't resist finding out for sure. Her hand trembled as she flipped open the lid. The diamond engagement ring stared up at her from the ivory cushion. Her hand trembled.

"Suzie? You okay? Did you find something to wear?"

Suzie glanced up at the door. She swallowed hard and tossed the ring back into the drawer. "Yes, I'll be right there."

"Okay."

Suzie changed into the t-shirt and wrapped up her blouse. Mary's skills with stain removal might just save it. When she stepped back out into the living area Paul stood up from the table.

"Wow, I have to say, Suzie, you looked gorgeous when you walked in here, but I think I like you even better in my t-shirt."

"Ha." Suzie smiled. "It is comfortable, I'll give it that. I'm sorry about spilling the wine."

"No problem. Let's just enjoy our meal."

171

Suzie sat back down at the table across from him, but she couldn't bring herself to look him in the eye. She knew that there was no way to avoid the truth now. She saw the ring with her own eyes. Paul was going to propose. The only positive thing was that the ring was still in the drawer. Maybe he bought it and was just waiting for the right moment. Maybe if she dropped big enough hints he would get the idea that she was not interested.

"You know, Paul, I do miss you when you're away, but sometimes I think that we're luckier than most."

"Oh?" He looked across the table at her. "Why is that?"

"Well, they say that absence makes the heart grow fonder. Yes, we have to spend time apart, but that makes us value our time together so much more."

"I guess that's true. But if it were up to me, I'd never leave your side."

Suzie took another bite of her food. She

wondered if Paul was the one who made sense in the scenario. If he could feel that way about her, why couldn't she feel that way about him?

"I love your company, Paul. But do you ever feel like if you don't get a little time to yourself you'll lose your mind?"

"Suzie. I'm alone on a boat a lot of the time. I get plenty of time to myself." He squinted at her. "Is there something you're trying to tell me?"

"No, I just..." The shrill ring of her cell phone interrupted her. She was relieved by the distraction. "I'm sorry, Paul, I have to take this."

"In the middle of dinner?" He raised an eyebrow.

"I know, I'm sorry. It's Louis. I asked him to look into some things for me earlier."

"If it's about the murder I understand. I'll be here." He smiled.

Suzie stood up and stepped out onto the deck of the boat. When she answered the phone Louis' voice was impatient.

"I didn't think that you were going to answer."

"I'm sorry I was in the middle of dinner with Paul."

"Sorry, I didn't mean to interrupt."

"It's okay. Did you find anything of interest?"

"Yes, I did. I think I did anyway. It looks like Leanne and Neil have quite a history. In fact Leanne's been arrested a few times and at least two of her arrests were directly related to her encounters with him."

"Really? What happened?"

"Leanne staged a protest over the encroachment of conservation land. She and her group made a human chain around the access point that the bulldozers needed to use. When Neil tried to convince them to move he and Leanne got involved in a shouting match that ended with her slapping him in the face."

"Wow. Poor Neil."

"Maybe. Another incident made it seem like

Neil was the aggressor. Leanne and a few like-minded friends hosted a sit-in to protest the hiring of a professor that was involved with the destruction of a foreign forest to make room for more houses. This had nothing to do with Neil that I can tell, however he still showed up at the protest and baited her into another argument. From what I understand he tried to drag her out of the room."

"Wait a minute. Why would he do that?"

"I'm not sure. The more I looked into the connection between the two the more it seemed rather paternal."

"So, Neil was playing the role of father?"

"Maybe there was something more between Priscilla and Neil than they were letting on?"

"Maybe." Suzie tapped the back of her phone. "It's honestly hard to say. The way they interacted when I saw them together was not anything near romantic."

"Maybe things went sour?"

"So, Neil decided to end it completely?" Suzie nodded slowly. "I guess that is a possibility. Or maybe Neil and Leanne worked together and killed her."

"Oh, that's a scandalous thought."

"Yes, it is." Suzie frowned. "Thanks for the information, Louis."

"You're welcome. I hope that it helps. Let me know if there's anything else that I can do."

"I will." Suzie hung up the phone. She turned around to step back inside the boat, but found Paul in the doorway.

"I just put everything away, I hope you don't mind."

"No, it's fine. I'm sorry that I interrupted dinner, twice."

He studied her for a long moment. Suzie shifted under his scrutiny. "Suzie, I don't care how many times dinner gets interrupted. But it really gets under my skin that you're not comfortable around me. I feel like ever since I got back you've been distant, or even worried. I know it's not about the case. So, what's going on? Did something else happen when I was out to sea?"

"No, nothing." She frowned. The last thing she wanted to do was lie to Paul, but she also didn't want to hurt his feelings. "I'm glad you're back. My mind is just in too many different places."

"If you say so." He cupped her cheeks with the weathered skin of his palms. "I just want you to know that you can tell me anything, Suzie. You don't need to hold anything back. I want us to be honest with each other, not because we have to be, but because we want to be."

"I want that too, Paul." Suzie searched his eyes. "I feel really lucky that we found each other."

"Good. That's all that matters to me." He hugged her. "Now, your mind may be in a million places, but I know one thing that will clear it right up."

"What's that?" He took her hand and led her

further out along the deck of the boat.

"Look up." He squeezed her hand. Suzie lifted her eyes to the sky. As she gazed at the star filled expanse her shoulders relaxed. She eased into Paul's arms. In that moment it struck her that she was exactly where she wanted to be, just as they were. She held on to him a little more tightly and hoped that nothing would ever change that.

Chapter Fifteen

On the drive home to Dune House Suzie thought about Leanne and Neil. Could they really have committed Priscilla's murder together? Could they be so ruthless?

Suzie stepped into Dune House to find Mary asleep on the couch. The luxury of not having any guests meant she could camp out in the living room. Despite her hesitation to live with Paul, she didn't regret sharing her space with Mary for a second. They understood each other in a way that only sisters could, even if they weren't blood related. Suzie tucked a blanket around Mary and set the book on the coffee table so that it wouldn't get bent.

Suzie walked down the hall to her room. She sat down on the edge of her bed and closed her eyes. She was relieved that Paul hadn't proposed yet, but after seeing that ring in his drawer she knew that it was only a matter of time. Maybe if she wasn't so distracted by the murder she would be able to think of a way to let him know that she had no interest in marriage. But she was mentally exhausted from the back and forth between suspects. She didn't think she was ever going to be able to communicate to Paul that she simply was not the marrying type.

Suzie sprawled out on her bed and hugged her pillow. She thought that maybe if the murder was solved her focus could return to Paul. Maybe if she made more of an effort to pay attention to him he wouldn't be so interested in changing what they had. She fell asleep with her heart heavy and her jaw tense. In the morning she woke to the shrill ring of her cell phone. Bleary-eyed she sat up in her bed and reached for it. She expected that it would be Paul, but when she answered it was Summer's gentle voice that greeted her.

"Morning Suzie. I'm sorry if I woke you."

"It's fine." Suzie glanced at the clock. She had slept quite a bit later than she usually did. "Did you get the test results?"

"Yes, I did. I'm afraid they weren't a match, Suzie. Wherever Priscilla was killed it was not in Redhawk River."

Suzie's heart dropped. A big part of her had already decided that was where Priscilla was killed. It hadn't really occurred to her that the test might not be a match. "That is surprising."

"I know. I really expected it to be a match. The preliminary results from the water in her lungs have come in. They indicate it was most likely tap water that she drowned in. She could have been killed anywhere that there was enough room to immerse her head. Maybe a bathtub."

"Wait a minute." Suzie's eyes widened. "Did you say bathtub?"

"Yes, I did. Why? Does that mean something to you?"

"It might. The night that Priscilla was killed the bathroom on her floor had puddles of water on it. Mary and I just assumed that someone forgot to bring a towel in there with them. Then

181

we noticed that the towels from Priscilla's room were missing, but we didn't think much of it, because guests take towels all the time. Or we thought perhaps they were mixed in with another load of laundry. I never considered that it could have had anything to do with Priscilla's death."

"It just might, Suzie. It's a place to start. I'll call Jason and send him over to take a look."

"Thanks." Suzie hung up the phone with a sinking feeling. Had the crime scene really been right under their noses the entire time? It seemed impossible to her and yet the truth was they never figured out where the missing towels were. She didn't think they were in any of Priscilla's luggage. She shuddered at the thought that Priscilla could have actually been killed in the bathtub. How could that have happened and no one know about it? Was it Stewart after all? Had Leanne followed her mother back to Dune House? She dressed and headed to the kitchen to find Mary.

"Morning." Mary smiled. "I'm glad you slept in."

"Mary, I think we have a serious problem." Suzie shook her head at the cup of coffee that Mary offered.

"What is it?"

"I think that Priscilla might have been killed here, in the bathroom."

"What?" Mary dropped the cup of coffee she held. The mug didn't break, but the coffee splashed all over the polished kitchen floor. "That's not possible."

Suzie grabbed a towel and began wiping up the mess. As she did she reminded Mary of the state they had found the bathroom in the night of Priscilla's death.

"That's terrible. I hope that's not the case." Mary frowned. Both were so engrossed in the conversation that they didn't even hear Jason enter the bed and breakfast. He was already in the kitchen when Suzie sensed another presence and glanced up to see him.

"Morning. What happened here?" Jason

looked at the remainder of the coffee on the floor.

"My hand slipped." Mary frowned.

"Need any help?" Jason reached for another towel.

"It's okay, Jason, I have it." Suzie straightened up. "Did Summer tell you about the bathroom?"

"She did, but it seems pretty unlikely that Priscilla was killed here. Still, we should check it out. Do you think the bathtub was used since that night?"

"I can't be sure but I don't think so. The rooms have small bathrooms with showers and both of our guests checked out pretty soon after Priscilla was found."

"Let's take a look."

"I'll show you to it." Mary led Jason down the hall. Suzie finished cleaning up the coffee, then joined them. When she arrived Jason had a flashlight pointed down into the drain of the bathtub.

"There's something in here."

"What?" Suzie frowned. "We keep it very clean."

"No, it's something shiny, metal. Hang on." He pulled a small knife out of his pocket and flipped it open. With careful movements he loosened the grate over the drain. When he slid it out of the way the hole was just large enough for him to fit his folded hand into. He pulled something out of the drain and held it out into the light.

"What is that?"

"It looks like a charm." Mary peered at it closely. "Like someone would wear on a bracelet."

"Is it what I think it is?" Suzie squinted at it. "I think it's a bird."

"It must be Priscilla's," Mary said.

"Well, we don't know that, yet," Jason said as he fished a small plastic bag out of another pocket. He dropped the charm into the plastic bag and sealed it. "I'm going to take another look." He

185

shone the flashlight beam down into the drain. As he searched it, Suzie noticed something strange about the tiles on the wall. One of them was cracked.

"Jason, look at that. I know that wasn't like that before. We do a maintenance check of the bathrooms before every check-in, including the tiles."

Jason looked up at the tile. He snapped a picture of it with his camera. "If we assume that Priscilla was killed in the bathtub the killer still had to move her body. It wouldn't be easy to sneak a body out the front door, so it looks like the killer pulled the body out through this window," Jason said as he looked at the window. "It looks like the window has been pulled off the track."

"I noticed that the other day, I was going to ask Paul to fix it," Suzie said.

Jason leaned forward and peered through the window. "Yes, that's not much of a drop. I'm going to go take a look."

Suzie and Mary followed after him as he rounded the house to the space under the window. Suzie remained close to Jason. When she paused behind him he gestured for her to back up a few steps

"Here it is. Right here." He crouched down and peered at the soil beneath the window. "See?"

Suzie crouched down beside him and Mary peered over her shoulder. There were deep grooves in the soil. "What caused that?" Suzie frowned.

"They're drag marks. If Priscilla was killed in the bathtub then she was pulled out through the window and dragged across the ground."

"Can we just follow the trail?" Mary glanced around. "Maybe we can find more evidence."

"No, it ends at the path. There's nothing more to find here. But I can tell you, this is very likely where the murder took place. I'm sorry, Suzie, but I'm going to have to have the bathroom sealed off until a crime tech team can comb through it."

"I understand. Of course, anything that is needed for the case."

"Suzie, you should be prepared for something else." He looked between her and Mary. "If the murder took place here at Dune House, as it seems that it did then you can expect that you and Mary will be added to the list of suspects."

"That's ridiculous. We had no reason to kill one of our own guests." Suzie shook her head.

"Sure you did. You had the same reason that everyone else who lives in this town did. You didn't want some large resort to take over Garber, so you decided to take matters into your own hands. Then there's the fact that even if you didn't commit the crime you might look compliant or involved, because it was done under your roof."

"Jason, you can't be serious."

"I'm just telling you what you can expect. It's not as if the rest of the town doesn't feel the same about the development on the beach. However, if it is confirmed that Priscilla was killed at Dune

188

House then the spotlight is going to be on you and Mary. The one good thing is that Stewart is already a good, solid suspect."

"What about Leanne?" Suzie frowned.

"Possibly. But when I spoke with her she didn't strike me as particularly strong."

"What do you mean?"

"I mean, if things happened the way we think they did then someone lowered Priscilla out of the window. She might have been a small woman, but it would still take a strong person to be able to do that."

Suzie's eyes suddenly widened. "What about the driver?'

"The driver?" Jason raised an eyebrow.

"Yes, Priscilla's driver. I saw him at Cheney's. He was meeting with Neil, which I thought was strange."

"Hm." Jason narrowed his eyes.

"And Leanne said that she sent Priscilla home

with her driver." Suzie groaned. "I forgot all about that."

"Well, Leanne told me that as well and I did speak with Conner," Jason said. "He confirmed that he drove Priscilla back to Dune House and dropped her off."

"Maybe Leanne did that as a way to hide her own actions." Suzie's brows knitted together. "She thought she could deflect blame because it would appear that Conner was the last person to see Priscilla alive."

"There's still the issue of how Priscilla's body got out the window."

"What if Conner and Leanne worked together?" Mary spoke up with a soft voice. "What if they bonded over their dislike of Priscilla and made the plan?"

"Then why would Conner be talking to Neil?" Suzie sighed.

Jason folded his arms. "Maybe Conner tried to play both sides. He offered to help Leanne, and then told Neil what happened?"

"If that's the case, why wouldn't Neil be using that information to get Leanne arrested? Why would he keep it to himself?"

"Maybe he plans to use it for leverage. To keep Leanne out of his business. Maybe it has something to do with the real estate deal." Mary shrugged.

"That's a good thought, Mary. I bet it has something to do with that. What do you think, Jason?"

"I think I'm going to have another conversation with Conner. I'll be sending over some crime scene techs, all right?"

"Okay." Suzie nodded and gritted her teeth. She didn't want to deal with police combing through the house, but she knew that she didn't have a choice. It made her feel uneasy to think that something horrible happened to Priscilla under their roof, but the evidence was there.

Suzie and Mary spent the afternoon catering for the crime scene techs with coffee and snacks. By early evening they had finished their work. Suzie didn't expect any more visitors for the day.

"Do you want to hit the hay early tonight, Suzie?"

Suzie was about to answer when she noticed a familiar face through the front window. When the front door opened Suzie held her breath. Seeing Leanne again was like seeing her for the first time, in a brand new light. She couldn't help but think of Leanne murdering her mother. It broke her heart and horrified her at the same time. Maybe it didn't happen at the river, but Suzie wasn't convinced that Leanne wasn't the one to take her mother's life.

"Hi." Leanne walked up to the front desk and looked from Mary to Suzie. "I'm here to pick up Benita."

"Oh?" Suzie looked over at the bird in the cage. "Are you sure that you're ready for her?"

"Yes. As much as my mother loved that bird, I know that she would want me to take care of her."

Mary frowned and met Suzie's eyes. Neither were completely comfortable with the idea of handing the bird over.

"Well, she has lots of food to go with her." Suzie picked up the cage.

"Don't worry about that, I've already bought my own supply. You were so kind to come see me after my mother's death. My mother was so impressed with both of you. I do hope that you plan to attend the funeral. Here is the information in case you do. It's a bit of a drive." She set down a small piece of paper. "It won't be anything extravagant, but I will do my best to honor her."

"You've had quite a change of heart." Suzie tilted her head to the side. "From what I understand you and your mother were barely speaking."

"We were. I am so grateful that we had the chance to reconnect. What's happened is horrible, and I plan to make sure that whoever committed this horrible act will pay for it. But I am so glad that we had the chance to finally see eye to eye. I think for a long time my mother thought that everything I did, I did out of pure spite. She didn't understand that I saw a need to protect the environment, that it was never about me being against her."

Suzie narrowed her eyes. From what she had read in Leanne's datebook she had a very different impression of Leanne's attitude towards her mother.

"So, in one evening you two were able to resolve all of that?" Suzie asked skeptically.

"Well, I think my mother was starting to appreciate family more as she got older. I guess maybe she was starting to change her perspective on a lot of things. I think she was more willing to listen to my opinion. Or maybe she realized that money really can't fix everything, sometimes damage is done and can't be repaired." Leanne frowned as she looked into Benita's cage. "My mother had a good spirit, it was just misguided at times."

"I'm very sorry for your loss, Leanne." Mary reached out and patted the back of her hand. "I'm sure it was a comfort to your mother to know that you two were able to reconnect."

"I hope so." Leanne blinked back tears. "I really do."

As Leanne carried the bird out through the door Mary sighed. "Poor girl."

"Maybe." Suzie arched an eyebrow. "Or maybe not."

Chapter Sixteen

The next day Suzie, Mary, and Wes drove to the funeral.

"Paul and Jason are going to meet us there," Mary said as she glanced at Wes.

"I heard that Jason took Conner in for questioning yesterday," Wes said.

"The driver?" Mary asked.

"Yes, Conner was refusing to give any information at all. Jason called me to see if I could give him some ways to get him to talk," Wes explained.

"I'm sure you were able to come up with something. You're very persuasive." Mary grinned. "I'd love to be a fly on the wall at one of your interrogations."

"Not me." Suzie laughed. "You're intense enough when you're not on duty."

"Yes, you certainly have a serious side." Mary

smiled at Wes who was about to protest.

"Here it is." Suzie pulled onto the gravel lot in front of a small church. As they stepped out of the car Suzie noticed there were quite a few other vehicles, and those vehicles were rather fancy. Mary slid one arm through Suzie's and one arm through Wes' and the three began to walk towards the church. When they stepped through the door they were greeted by soft music, faint floral scents, and the commotion of people having multiple conversations. The wooden pews were filled with people that could have been models or movie stars. It was clear that Priscilla had quite an elite circle of friends. Suzie studied each face that she saw. She didn't want to forget a single detail. In her experience the truth could come out at funerals.

With the way they were struggling to solve the murder it would be a very good thing if some new evidence surfaced. However, the prim and proper behavior of the people around her made her think that there was not much chance of that. They took their seats near the back of the church.

"I'm going to check for Jason and Paul." Wes turned back towards the door.

"We'll save your seats." Suzie made sure there was space for three more in the pew. After a few minutes the noise of conversation settled to a quiet buzz.

"They're starting." Mary patted Suzie's hand and tilted her head towards the minister at the front of the church.

"Okay." Suzie sat up straight in her chair. "Watch for anyone showing up after it starts, or stepping out in the middle." She glanced around in search of Paul, but didn't see him, Wes, or Jason.

"I'll take the left, you take the right."

"Good." Suzie scanned the chairs. She spotted Neil at the front of the room. He glared at Leanne who sat in a chair beside the minister. As the minister went through a rehearsed, but heartfelt speech, Suzie looked around again for Paul. She turned her attention back to the front of the room as Leanne stood up and the minister sat down.

"First, I want to thank all of you for coming. Some of you may not even know who I am. I'm Priscilla's daughter, Leanne. My mother and I haven't always seen eye to eye. Many of you know that. Despite all of the times I have claimed differently, she was an amazing mother. We wasted many years through lack of communication and misunderstanding each other. I will always regret that. But as a little girl she always made sure I had everything I needed. I still close my eyes and expect to hear her call me Pumpkin."

Suzie's eyes widened at the nickname. She looked over at Mary who nodded. It was the same word that Benita repeated over and over. Was it possible that the bird was attempting to name Priscilla's killer, the last person she saw? Suzie stared at Leanne as she continued the eulogy. All of her words were beautiful, touching, but Suzie didn't believe them. Suzie was starting to believe that Leanne had killed her own mother. The tension must have been visible in her expression because Mary reached out and touched her hand.

"Not here, Suzie. Not here."

Suzie nodded. She didn't even hear the rest of Leanne's eulogy as her head pounded with the revelation of the woman's nickname. She did however notice when Neil stood up from his seat and walked right down the middle of the aisle and out of the church. She watched the door shut behind him.

"What was that all about?" Mary whispered.

"I'm not sure." Suzie frowned. "But it certainly was rude."

As the ceremony came to an end, Suzie stood up.

"I want to find Jason, maybe he's with Paul and Wes. I want them to know about Leanne's nickname."

"I think they're over there." Mary pointed out a group of men gathered near the door. As Suzie approached them she noticed that Summer stood beside Jason.

"Jason, I need to speak to you."

"What is it?" Jason turned towards her.

"Somewhere a bit more private."

"All right. Excuse me for a second." He met Summer's eyes. "I'll be right back."

Suzie led him out through the front of the church. When she was sure they were isolated she turned to face him. "Did you hear Priscilla's nickname for Leanne?"

"Yes, I did. Pumpkin? That's a pretty common nickname isn't it?"

"Yes, it is. It's also what Priscilla's bird has been saying non-stop, ever since Priscilla was killed. Don't you think it's possible that the bird might be trying to tell us something?"

"I'm sorry? The bird? You think that a bird is telling us who the killer is?"

"I think it's possible. Priscilla loved that bird,

and she took it wherever she could with her. It must have heard what she said and seen the people she spent time with."

"Suzie, it's still a bird. You can't be serious. It's not as if that can be evidence."

"Jason, you don't have to be so dismissive. I think it's possible that the bird witnessed something to do with the murder. Leanne is already a solid suspect, this just adds fuel to the fire. Don't you think?"

"I think that you're letting this case get way too deep into your head. Priscilla is dead, and yes Leanne may have been involved, but a bird that says Pumpkin is not going to sway any judge or jury. In fact, if I even try to enter it in as potential evidence I'll be laughed right out of the police station."

"I see what you're saying." Suzie frowned. "I guess I am getting desperate. I just want to make sure there's enough evidence to keep Leanne here."

"Well, I plan to take her in for further questioning. Unfortunately, she is planning on leaving town later tonight so I need to do it as soon as the funeral is finished. I spoke to Conner again and he informed me of some very interesting facts about Leanne's history with her mother, including the several times he's witnessed the two engaged in screaming matches. He also said that when he picked up Priscilla she was visibly upset. He tried to find out what was wrong and she refused to talk about it. When he dropped her off, he offered to walk her in, and she refused."

"That's not unusual though, Conner told me that Priscilla never allowed him inside."

"Maybe. It doesn't sound to me like the two made up the way Leanne claimed."

Suzie nodded. "Leanne told me yesterday that her mother seemed to be appreciating family more in her old age and she seemed to be opening her mind a little."

"Or maybe Leanne is lying. I don't know. The way Conner described her was pretty ruthless," Jason said.

"And you don't think Conner was involved and could be lying?"

"He could be but I don't think so. Once I got him talking he actually seemed quite open about things. He said he was meeting with Neil because he had offered him work as his driver."

"You believe him?"

"It all adds up. At the moment Leanne is our best suspect."

"So, you have enough to arrest her?" Suzie asked.

"Not yet, I'm just going to question her further, but it might lead to an arrest. She was in town at the time of the murder. She was seen with the victim not long before her death. She has all kinds of motive."

"But what about Stewart? He saw Priscilla return to Dune House alone," Suzie said.

"Stewart isn't exactly a reliable witness. However, even if he did see her return alone, that doesn't mean that Leanne didn't meet her there. Also, I want to try and get a search warrant for Leanne's room to see if there is any evidence that she was involved." Suzie was relieved to hear that because if Jason could search the room then he would probably get to see the entries in Leanne's datebook and he would have more evidence.

"Is there any evidence in Priscilla's phone records?"

"No. She didn't receive any calls that night. That's the frustrating part. Stewart looked like the perfect culprit because he was right there. The only problem is, there's no motive that we can find. He had nothing to gain from killing Priscilla. Even with his history of assault I find it hard to believe that he would kill Priscilla for fun."

"So, you're not going to question him?"

"Once we catch up with him we will. But I'm hoping to get enough information from Leanne to clear him entirely. I think this is one of the only murder cases where I've had so many good suspects. One of them did this, and I am determined to figure it out soon."

"You will!" Suzie said with confidence.

"I hope so." Jason frowned as he looked towards the church. Leanne exited alone with her gaze towards the ground. "Time to get to the bottom of all of this." He strode towards Leanne. Suzie followed right behind him. She wanted to see Leanne's reaction.

"Leanne Kay, I need to take you in for further questioning concerning the murder of Priscilla Kane."

"What?" Leanne looked from Jason to Suzie. "You think I had something to do with the murder. That's not true. You can't accuse me of something that isn't true. You can't."

Mary walked up beside Suzie. "What's going on?"

Suzie pulled her back slightly and shushed

her.

"Ms. Kay, I am not accusing you of anything, I just want to get to the bottom of this. It would be best if you cooperate." Jason met her eyes. "I don't want to have to forcibly bring you in for questioning. I don't want to have to handcuff you here. If you come with me willingly, I won't have to."

"How can you do this to me? How could you think that I would kill my own mother?" Leanne looked into Suzie's eyes. "I wouldn't do that. You know that I wouldn't. You have to know."

Suzie glanced away from her. Jason led Leanne away. When they reached the patrol car Leanne turned back to look at Suzie again.

"The bird. She is still at the motel. Please, will you take care of Benita? If anything happens to that bird I will have really failed my mother."

"We'll take care of her, Leanne." Mary offered her a sympathetic smile. "We'll make sure that she's safe."

"Let's go." Jason guided her into the car.

"Why did you say that we would take care of that bird?" Suzie looked over at her.

"Because we will. Someone needs to. Dune House could use a pet, even if it's not permanent." Mary frowned. "If Leanne didn't do this she'll be out to take her back. It's the least we can offer, Suzie."

"Do you really think we should be offering her anything?" Suzie crossed her arms. "She killed her own mother."

"Allegedly." Mary shook her head. Wes walked up to both of them. He put a hand on Mary's shoulder. "It's not the bird's fault."

"Are you okay?" Wes asked.

"I will be," Mary said.

"Suzie?" Wes looked at her.

"I'm okay." Suzie closed her eyes. "I just can't believe that a daughter could do that to her mother."

"It is a tragic case." Wes frowned as Paul walked over to them.

"Where have you been?" Suzie looked at Paul with surprise. "You missed the entire ceremony."

"I'm sorry. Wes and I were having a conversation with Jason."

"The three of you?" Mary looked at them both. "About what?"

"Uh, well, that's personal." Wes cleared his throat.

"Yes. It was boy talk." Paul winked at Suzie. Suzie's throat grew dry. Was Paul talking to them about the ring? She hoped that wasn't the case.

"Can we go home now?" Mary leaned her head against Wes' shoulder. "This day has worn me out, I think I need a little beach time."

"Anytime." He wrapped his arm around her waist. "Suzie, will you join us on the beach?"

"I don't think so." Suzie met Paul's eyes. "Something about this case has left me on edge. I think I just need some time to think it all through."

"I've seen it far too many times. When it comes to murder within the family there is never anything but sadness." Wes drew his lips into a tight line.

"I couldn't imagine either of my children ever being angry enough at me to cause me harm." Mary sighed. "It breaks my heart to think that things were so horrible between Leanne and Priscilla."

"Love can make you do the strangest things." Suzie sighed.

"No, it can't, Suzie." Paul took her hand in his. "Love doesn't make you do that. Hate, resentment, anger, can all make you do that. But love never makes you do that."

"Maybe. But not everyone is cut out for love, or uh, marriage," Suzie said.

Mary cleared her throat. Paul narrowed his eyes. Wes let out a quiet whistle. "I guess we'd better get going," Wes said.

"Suzie, I have my car if you want to ride with me." Paul gave her hand a light squeeze. "We could get lunch, or take a walk."

"Oh no, thanks Paul. I think I just need a little time to myself." Paul held her gaze for a long moment.

"Are you sure?"

"Yes, I'm sorry. You don't mind do you?"

He studied her. "If that's what you want, I don't mind."

"Great." Suzie smiled. Despite Paul's flexible response she detected a hint of frustration in his voice. A twinge of guilt summoned a subtle ache in her heart, but it didn't make her change her mind. "Thanks Paul." She leaned close and kissed his cheek. As she walked back towards the car she could feel Paul's eyes trained on her back. Her stomach twisted with regret. The last thing she wanted to do was hurt Paul. But she had no idea what she would say when he popped the question.

She hoped that if she kept avoiding being alone with him she'd come up with the perfect response. Once they were in the car together with Wes, Mary glanced over at her.

"Are you okay, Suzie?"

"Sure." Suzie kept her eyes on the road.

"It just seems like maybe you're having a hard time with something."

"Mary, I'm fine."

"You don't seem fine. Does she seem fine to you, Wes?" Mary looked in the backseat at Wes.

"Uh, I, well." Wes frowned.

"I'm fine, really. I'm just nervous I guess."

"Nervous about what?" Mary asked.

"I found something on Paul's boat. An engagement ring. You were right, Mary, I think he's going to propose."

Wes coughed in the backseat.

"And you really don't want that do you?" Mary frowned.

"No. Honestly, I've tried to get used to the idea, to open my mind to it, but it's just not the right thing for me."

"So, just tell him that, Suzie. Paul will understand."

"Would you understand, Wes?" Suzie looked in the rearview mirror at him. Wes' cheeks were red. He looked away from her.

"How I would react doesn't matter. But Paul seems like the type of guy that respects honesty. I think the hardest thing for a man is to be lied to by someone he trusts. So, if you want my opinion, I agree with Mary, you should just tell him. I'm sure if you two talk it through things will clear right up."

"Maybe." Suzie bit into her bottom lip. She wasn't prepared to get married, but she really wasn't prepared to lose Paul.

Chapter Seventeen

When Suzie, Mary and Wes pulled up to Dune House there was a car in the parking lot that Suzie didn't recognize.

"I wonder who that is." Suzie parked the car and stepped out. As the three approached Dune House Suzie saw that the door was open. Her heart pounded. Had she left it open? She didn't think so.

"Mary, didn't we lock up when we left?"

"I'm not sure." Mary frowned.

"Let me go in first." Wes pushed past the two women and jogged up the steps and across the porch. Suzie and Mary hurried after him. When Wes stepped inside a man at the front desk turned around with a frown.

"Do you work here? I've been waiting here forever."

Suzie moved past Wes. The man was tall, thin,

and carried a soft-sided briefcase. He didn't appear to be a threat, but Suzie knew better than to judge a person by looks.

"Excuse me, can anyone help me here?" He tapped his palm on the desk. "Does anyone even work here?"

"I'm sorry I'll be right there." Suzie left Mary and Wes and walked up to the front desk. "I apologize, we weren't expecting another guest."

"I'm not a guest. I'm here on behalf of Priscilla Kane's estate. I'm her real estate lawyer. I need to get the paperwork that was in her possession."

"I'm sure you're aware of what happened to Priscilla?" Suzie said.

"I am. It's quite unfortunate. But the deal stands. I was awaiting the fax of the final signed paperwork. Since she obviously can't fax it now I need to get the paperwork from her room."

"What about her daughter?" Suzie frowned. "Shouldn't she be the one to handle all of this?"

"Absolutely not. She would never agree to the

deal. As long as the paperwork is signed the deal stands. Now, please let me retrieve it from the room."

"The police should have all the paperwork," Suzie said.

"Well, they don't have this particular piece, so it must still be in her room. So, you must let me get it," he said with authority.

Suzie glanced over at Mary and Wes. She knew that the locals would be infuriated if the deal stood despite Priscilla's death. She felt uneasy as she looked up at the man before her.

"I'll need some proof of identity."

"Sure." He pulled his wallet out of his back pocket and withdrew his driver's license. "There you are. Now?"

"I'll just need to make a copy." She carried the license with her as she walked over to Wes and Mary. "It looks like there's been a wrinkle. This man, Tyler Grants is here to pick up the paperwork to finalize the deal."

"But how can he do that if Priscilla is dead?" Mary's eyes widened.

"As long as the paperwork is signed then the deal stands." Suzie shook her head.

"The police should have it in evidence," Wes said.

"Apparently, they don't," Suzie said. "I'm trying to stall him, but there's nothing that I can do about it."

"We could get to the paperwork first and hide it, or burn it even," Mary suggested.

"No." Wes put his hand on Mary's shoulder. "You can't do that, Mary. If you do you, Suzie, and Dune House could be sued. It's not something you should risk."

"Then what? Garber is going to be destroyed after all?" Mary asked.

"I doubt it's in the room if the police didn't find it. Even if it is maybe she didn't sign the paperwork." Wes shrugged. "Maybe Leanne was telling the truth and she had a change of heart."

"Maybe. But I doubt it. Priscilla was quite confident in her decision the last time I spoke with her. I'm sure the paperwork was ready to go. That is even more reason why Leanne would have taken drastic action to protect the seabirds," Suzie said. "Maybe Priscilla told her that the deal was done and Leanne thought the only option was to kill her mother."

"Then she obviously didn't know that it wouldn't matter." Mary frowned. "All right. I'll show him to the room. Wes, will you accompany me?"

"Yes, of course."

"I'm going to go to the motel and get Benita," Suzie said. "I'm sure that no one has tended to her, and since you've decided she's our new, or at least temporary, mascot, we're going to want her to be healthy."

"Thanks Suzie." Mary smiled. Suzie grabbed her purse and headed for the door.

As she walked to the car she thought about the

shock in Leanne's eyes when she had found out that her mother had been murdered. It bothered her. It wasn't something that could be easily faked. But if her reaction had been genuine then could that mean that Leanne was innocent?

The entire drive to the motel Suzie thought through what she knew about the murder. Leanne had motive to murder her mother. She expressed her hatred openly. On the night of her death, Leanne was with her for a considerable amount of time. When Priscilla left the restaurant she looked drunk, but maybe that was because Leanne drugged her or maybe simply because of her broken heel. The one piece of the puzzle that didn't fit was how Leanne got her mother's body out of Dune House. Suzie parked the car in front of Leanne's room, but when she got out, she headed straight for the office. She gave the bell on the front desk two sharp swats. The tinny sound summoned Maurice from the back room.

"You again. Come to accuse me of yet another murder?"

"No, not at all. I'm here to collect Benita. I need the key to Leanne's room, please."

"You have a warrant?" Maurice sucked his teeth.

"Maurice, I really don't have time for this. I need to get to the bird before it croaks."

"All right. I don't want to have to deal with that." He snatched a key from behind the desk and handed it over. "I know what's in there, so no stealing."

"What's in there?" Suzie clutched the key tightly in her hand.

"Towels, soap." He shrugged.

"Oh, okay. I'll try to restrain myself." Suzie smirked and shook her head as she walked away. When she returned to Leanne's room she slid the key into the lock. It was a lot easier than climbing in through the window that was for sure. She turned the knob and stepped inside. She left the door open so that it would be easy to carry the cage back through the door. As soon as she walked in Benita began to chirp.

"Pumpkin!"

"Yes, I know, Pumpkin's with the police." Suzie peered through the bars of the cage at the bird. "Let's get you home." She started to pick up the cage, but noticed that the bird's water bottle was empty. She opened the door of the cage and pulled out the water bottle. As she did her cell phone rang. She paused and pulled her phone out of her pocket. She saw that it was Mary calling.

"Hello?"

"Suzie, I know you're getting Benita, but I wanted to let you know what we found."

"What is it?"

"The paperwork Priscilla was supposed to fax to her lawyer was found in evidence. Jason managed to locate it. After the lawyer couldn't find it in her room he called the police again. It was tucked away in a special section of her laptop case that the police didn't notice so they didn't find it originally. But the lawyer was determined it had to be somewhere. After the lawyer told Jason about the compartment he found it. All of the documents she signed were crossed out."

"What do you mean?"

"I mean the paperwork was ready to go to finalize the deal, but Priscilla crossed it all out making it invalid."

"Are you sure it was Priscilla?"

"She left her initials on each page. It's possible they were faked, but if they were, why would Leanne make the paperwork so difficult to find?"

"So, you think Leanne was telling the truth about her mother having a change of heart?"

"It sure seems that way. If Leanne was able to convince her mother to change her mind, then why would she kill her mother?"

"That wouldn't make any sense at all. I think you might be right," Suzie said. "Maybe she had nothing to do with her mother's death after all."

"Maybe. Are you headed back to Dune

House?"

"Not just yet. I am refilling Benita's water and then I'll be on my way. Poor Leanne. If this is true she's been arrested in error."

"I know. Hopefully Jason will think this is enough to release her."

"If it's not Leanne then Jason will have to look at the other suspects."

"I think we need to look more closely at one person."

"Who?" Mary didn't answer. "Mary?" When Mary didn't respond Suzie looked at her phone. She saw that the call had dropped. With a sigh she set down her phone on the table beside the birdcage. She was better off getting back to Dune House and discussing things with Mary there. She walked over to the sink to fill the water bottle. When she turned on the water Benita began to shriek.

"Relax Benita, I'm getting it right now." Suzie shook her head. "I don't think I'm a bird person."

Her mind returned to the information that Mary had just given her. If the killer wasn't Leanne, then who was it? Who would lose the most if the resort didn't go ahead?

When Suzie turned back towards the cage a shadow fell across the room. It drew her attention to the window. For an instant she froze as a sensation coursed through her of being watched. The water bottle fell onto the floor. Benita shrieked even louder. Suzie was sure that she saw someone duck away from the window. Were they looking for Leanne or had she been followed by the real killer? She hurried out of the motel room to try to catch whoever peeked in the window. Maybe if she did she could find the final piece of the puzzle and save Jason the headache. Who had something against Priscilla? The driver?

Suzie walked around the side of the motel and noticed a car parked beside and partially behind the dumpster. It looked like someone had gone to a lot of trouble to try to hide the vehicle. As Suzie stepped closer she recognized the car right away.

It was the same car that Neil Runkin drove up to Dune House in. She thought he had left town days ago so what was his car doing at the motel? Suzie glanced around to see if anyone might be nearby. When she saw that no one was around she stepped closer to the car. She wanted to be sure that she was not mistaken. The car looked just like the one that Neil drove, but it could have been a different one.

As she walked around behind the car to check the license plate she noticed something strange. The corner of a thick, white towel stuck out of the trunk. It partially blocked the license plate. Suzie picked up the corner of the towel to see the full plate. When she did she brushed her fingers over the tag which had the letters DH embroidered on it. Suzie froze. That stood for Dune House. Why would Neil have one of the towels from Dune House in his trunk? Her heart began to race as she remembered all of the missing towels and the trail of water out of the bathroom.

As her mind began to piece together what

might have happened to Priscilla she grew dizzy. She stumbled back from the trunk and right into the chest of someone who stood behind her. She let out a shriek as she spun around to face the person. Neil scowled at her as he grabbed her hard by the neck with one hand. "You just had to snoop didn't you?"

Suzie struggled against him. She heard the subtle beep of a key fob being pressed then the click of the trunk popping open. Before she could take a breath the hard edge of the open trunk struck the back of her knees. In that moment she realized she was in real trouble. She tried to get her bearings enough to fight her way out of the trunk, but Neil swung her legs over the edge and shoved her down on top of a pile of towels. Without a single word of explanation he slammed the trunk shut.

Chapter Eighteen

Darkness filled every corner of the small space. Suzie didn't dare to take a breath as she waited for what felt like hours, but was just a few minutes. Only when she heard the engine start up did she begin to scream. Through the thick metal of the car she was certain that no one could hear her shrieks for help. After some time she stopped in order to conserve her energy. There was no chance of rescue, she had to focus on how to escape. Suzie tried to see in the dark trunk, but it was a struggle.

The damp towels created a musty scent that made it hard for her to breathe. She could feel the movement of the car as Neil drove along. How could she have missed the fact that Neil was the one who killed Priscilla? He had the most to lose from her changing her mind. Without Priscilla's support the deal would never go through. The only question on her mind was whether Leanne was in on it as well. Had Neil and Leanne forged some kind of alliance in an attempt to end Priscilla's life? Her muscles felt every bump and curve in the road. Her jaw clenched with fear.

Suzie tried to work out where Neil might be headed. Would she end up at the beach, tossed into the water as Priscilla had been? Would her body be found in a few days with no explanation of what had happened to her?

Suzie squeezed her eyes shut and balled her hands into fists as she mustered all her energy to remain strong. She had to figure a way out of the predicament she had landed herself in. She shifted in the trunk so that her feet would be available to thrust upward into a kick. The only opportunity for escape that she would likely have was the moment that Neil opened the trunk. When the car finally came to a stop Suzie held her breath. What would Neil do with her? Her heart raced. She thought of Mary and what might happen to her once she was gone. Sure, she would manage, but it wouldn't be the same. Suzie knew she only had a few minutes to think of something to do.

She grabbed what towels she could find and balled them up together. The more she balled them up the heavier the damp towels became. She heard the door of the car creak open. Then footsteps as they rounded the car. Suzie clutched the ball of towels tightly in her hands. When Neil popped the trunk she waited for him to lean in. When he did she slammed the towels right into his face. Neil stumbled back with surprise. She swung her legs over the side of the trunk and jumped out. Right away she was hit with the scent of the sea. She was near the ocean, near enough to hear the crash of the waves.

Suzie wanted more than anything to flee, but she had no idea in which direction to go in. The car was parked in an empty parking lot of what looked like an abandoned building. She could run towards the street or she could run towards the ocean. If she ran towards the street she had no idea what she would run into. If she ran towards the ocean she presumed that it would eventually lead her back to Dune House. She decided to take her chances in the sand. As she ran she heard Neil shout from behind her.

"You're not going to get away from me! Get back here!" Suzie ignored his warning and ran as fast as she could. As soon as she reached the sand she realized her mistake. The beach was deserted. There wasn't a tourist or a local in sight. She had no idea where Neil had driven her, but it was nowhere near Dune House. With her decision already made she had no choice but to keep going. Her feet sank deep into the thick sand. Within moments she left her shoes behind.

Neil's heavy breath was only a few steps behind her. She had no idea if he would get tired before her. As hard as her heart pounded she wasn't sure how much longer she would be able to run. In the distance she saw a beach umbrella. It was bright yellow and blue. She used it as her focus as she ran as hard and as fast as she could. One slip in the sand and Neil would be upon her.

Then there would be no escape. The beach umbrella glimmered in the sunlight. When she was close enough that she thought someone might hear, she risked the breath in her lungs by screaming.

"Help! Please help me!"

She reached the beach umbrella, but the chair beneath it was empty. There was no house to run to, no resort or even a restaurant. It was just a beach umbrella in the middle of an isolated beach that someone might have abandoned long ago. Winded, Suzie tried to run again, but her legs trembled too hard to carry her. She collapsed into the sand. A spray of sand struck the back of her head as Neil skidded to a stop right behind her. She knew then, that she was not going to escape. She might have even made Neil's life easier by wearing herself out.

"Thanks for the work out." Neil chuckled. "I needed that." He reached down and grabbed her under the arms. Suzie made a mild attempt to wriggle free of his grip. She became aware that he didn't seem the least bit concerned about being seen. That meant that he already knew there was no one around to see him. Suzie closed her eyes and waited for her body to be tossed into the water. Instead Neil pulled her back towards the building.

"Let me go, Neil. Let me go." Suzie looked up at him as he tugged her right through the door of the building. "Please. I won't tell anyone. I won't say a word. Just let me go."

"I'm sorry, I can't do that." He scowled at her. "It's not as if I forced you to get involved in all of this. This is not my fault."

"Please, Neil." He tossed her down on the concrete floor. Suzie struggled to pull herself up to her feet. She was exhausted. Neil grabbed her arm firmly.

"Look, this isn't personal. My life is simple. It's all about numbers and profit. I can't let anything get in my way. I lost a lot of money on this property and I have some very dangerous people upset with me. I need this deal to go through. I have a lot riding on it. You are going to be a casualty to a great development for Garber, if that gives you any peace."

"Just let me go, Neil. If I figured this out, then others will, too. Do you want two murders hanging over your head?"

"Eh, what's one more?" He pushed her towards the wall of the empty building. "By the time they find you everyone will have forgotten about Priscilla. No one will put two and two together."

Suzie's heart lurched. Was he right? Just as he pulled the door closed behind him, Suzie heard something in the distance. She drew a sharp breath at the sound. Was it possible or was it just her imagination? The thought was swept from her mind as Neil approached her.

"I have to make a phone call. Your presence interrupted a very important meeting. Once that's settled, I'll take care of you." He turned away from her as he pulled out his cell phone. Suzie looked around for anything that she could strike him with. There was nothing but dust and sand on the floor. On one wall a large poster was worn and weathered. It depicted what appeared to be a large resort.

It struck her that Neil was holding her captive in the remains of a failed beach resort. No wonder there was no one around. He probably owned everything she could see. Maybe, just maybe, if someone noticed she was missing and figured out by some miracle that Neil took her, they would think to look for her there. But by the time all of that happened, she was sure it would be far too late for her. She heard snippets of Neil's conversation about the development deal. It took a callous man to settle business matters while his future murder victim waited for his attention.

Suzie summoned all of her strength and started to stumble towards an open window. It was a bit too high for her to just climb through, but she had to try. As her feet shuffled along the concrete she noticed that Neil's voice no longer filtered through the air. Her heart sank as she realized that he had hung up the phone. Her futile attempt to reach the window ended before she even made it a few steps. He pinned her back against the wall. However, as she was shoved she heard the sound again. She was certain that the chirp was familiar. "Pumpkin! Pumpkin!"

Neil scowled and looked towards the window. "That damn bird!" His grip tightened on one of her arms. He clamped his other hand over her mouth. "Don't make a sound, understand?" When he met her eyes Suzie nodded. She knew that he was distracted by the bird, she could only hope that would give her an advantage. The bird landed on the windowsill of the open window. When Suzie saw her she wondered if it was all an illusion. But Neil's tightened grasp told her that he saw the bird, too.

"Pumpkin! Pumpkin!" The bird shrieked. All at once Suzie knew that the bird wasn't saying pumpkin at all. Benita was saying Runkin. Since pumpkin was more common that was just what people heard. The entire time the bird knew who the killer was. If only Suzie had paid attention she might have been more cautious around Neil's car. But she knew better than that. Nothing would have stopped her from investigating.

"I'm going to get rid of that bird once and for all." He kept one hand clamped over Suzie's mouth and used his other hand to draw his gun. He pointed it towards the bird on the windowsill.

"No!" Suzie cried out against his palm. With her hands free she grabbed at the hand that held the weapon. Neil's hand dipped in reaction to the pressure. An explosion filled the air. It rocked Suzie's senses to the point of stopping her heart and stealing her breath. She squeezed his wrist hard to try to get the weapon to drop, but he easily pushed her back against the wall. When he did she caught sight of the bullet hole in the baseboard beneath the window. Benita was gone, but not likely harmed. However, without the bird to focus on, Neil turned the gun back on Suzie.

"You shouldn't have done that. I'm getting tired of this fight with you. I think I'm just going to put an end to all of this right this second."

"No Neil, don't. This isn't the way to solve things. It wasn't the way to deal with Priscilla either. You know that. You just didn't take the time to think it through. You let your emotions get the better of you."

"Keep quiet! You have no idea what you're talking about! Priscilla let that stupid girl get into her head! That wasn't my fault either."

"You took a mother from her daughter, you..."

Neil scowled at her with such intensity that Suzie winced. "You have no idea what I have endured for both of those women. When Leanne was a girl I tried. She was a wayward, strong-willed kid with no father to guide her. I stepped up as a father figure for her. I taught her everything I knew about business. I gave her an education that was priceless. Did she thank me? No. Of course not. She used everything I taught

237

her to try to take me down in the public eye. What kind of ruthless person does that?"

Suzie just looked at him without responding. If he was talking then at least he wasn't pulling the trigger.

"Then Priscilla, my sweet, stupid Priscilla, she got caught up in her daughter's psychosis. For years I managed to keep the two of them apart, but in the end Leanne managed to creep inside of Priscilla's head. That's when I knew that I had no choice but to end it. Priscilla came to me and said she wanted out of the deal, the deal that was going to make us both millionaires, the deal that I've been working towards my entire life. How could I ever let that happen? I mixed her a drink. I spiked it, then I took care of things. She never felt a thing. She never knew what happened. I was merciful."

"There is nothing merciful about murder!" Suzie met his eyes with fury in her own. "You're a selfish, terrible person, Neil, and no amount of justification is going to change that."

"I'm okay with being who I am." He shrugged. "I don't have a choice in the matter. It's my nature. This building we're in now was supposed to be my ticket to success. It was going to be the jewel of the coast. Instead, the deal was stopped because of an issue with turtles. Can you believe it? Rats in shells cost me every penny of my investment. It took years of small buys to build my fortune again. Then I turned around and sank it into this deal. I will not let anything stop it from going through. Not Priscilla, not you, and not Leanne if she gets it in her head to try to stop me. I will go and pick off every one of those seabirds myself if I need to."

"It's crazy that you can feel this way, Neil. These people were like your family, and this is how you treated them? It's disgusting. You have to see that none of this can be right. You're sick, and you need help, Neil."

"It's all over for you now. Money is power, and I don't need family if I'm successful. You consider that woman you live with to be your family don't

239

you? How about that fisherman you date? And your long lost cousin, a police officer no less? But who showed up to save you? Just some belligerent bird. That's how far family gets you, Suzie. I'm doing you a favor by ending things for you before you're forced to learn that lesson."

He raised the gun and pointed it towards her face. Suzie flinched and turned away but she knew there was no real way to avoid the bullet.

An explosion filled the air. Suzie's entire body jolted. She felt a heavy weight against her chest. It didn't hurt as much as she thought it would. She braced herself for her final breath. But she didn't feel any pain, or have any difficulty breathing. In fact her heart pounded so hard that she was sure it was getting stronger.

"Suzie? Suzie!"

She knew that voice, it was Jason. She opened her eyes. Benita perched on the windowsill right in front of her. Suzie realized that the heaviness against her chest was Neil's weight slumped against her. The gun in his hand clattered to the cement floor.

"Jason?" Suzie cleared her throat. She was shocked that she could speak.

"Hold on." Jason tugged at Neil until he crumpled to the ground. Suzie could see that he'd been shot in the shoulder. His eyes were closed, but his face crinkled in pain. "Are you okay? Are you hurt?" Jason looked her over from head to toe. "I have the medics on their way in."

"I'm okay, Jason. I think I'm okay." She looked up at him with wide eyes. "You saved me."

Behind Jason, Kirk rushed in followed by a few uniformed officers. Jason looked into her eyes.

"Suzie. I'm sorry it took me so long to get here." Without awaiting a response Jason put his arms around her and held her close. Only then did Suzie realize that tears streamed down her cheeks.

"I'm so glad you came." She hugged him in

return with her arms so tight around him that she wondered if he could breathe.

"Let's get you outside." Jason guided her past the paramedics that tended to Neil. Kirk retrieved Neil's gun, then stood watch over him. The sunlight greeted Suzie as she stepped outside. There, in the parking lot, strenuously restrained by two officers was Mary. She pushed past the officers and rushed towards her.

"I know you told me to wait here, Jason, but I heard the gun shot, and I..." Mary hugged Suzie. "Are you okay? Please tell me that you're not hurt."

"I'm not hurt," Suzie said.

"I will kill him!" Mary exclaimed. "I will kill him with my bare hands, Jason, you might need to put me in handcuffs."

"Oh Mary." Suzie smiled through tear-filled eyes. "You're not going to kill anyone."

"You don't know that. I might. I sure want to." Mary pursed her lips. "I got a call from Maurice.

He said you let the bird loose and it was shrieking about pumpkins. I knew you would never do that so I tried to call your cell phone. When you didn't answer I knew something was wrong. Wes and I drove to the motel. We found your purse, your phone, and an open birdcage. Benita was shrieking just like Maurice said she was. Wes threatened Maurice for information, but Maurice insisted he only gave you the key and hadn't seen you since. Benita kept flying around the dumpster. Wes noticed an oil stain on the ground. He saw the same oil stain at Dune House and put two and two together and we presumed that it was probably from Neil's car. Since it was fresh, we thought perhaps he saw what happened or was involved. After the paperwork we found, Neil was already our best suspect."

"And then Benita led you all the way here?" Suzie's eyes widened.

"No, not exactly." Mary smiled. "Jason ordered a 'be on the lookout' for Neil's vehicle to be sent out to all patrol cars. Since Neil's car is pretty noticeable it didn't take long to track it down. Wes has a police radio so we came here straight away. I did let Benita out of her cage when we got here hoping that she might distract Neil. I had no idea that she would land on the windowsill like that."

"If she hadn't I might not have made it out of there. Neil admitted that he killed Priscilla and Leanne had nothing to do with it."

"We heard." Wes nodded as he walked up to them. "Everything is going to be fine. Once Neil is treated he'll be headed to prison, and that will be the last time he can hurt anyone."

"What about the real estate deal?" Suzie frowned.

"It won't go ahead. The paperwork was never sent and because Priscilla crossed out everything it can't be used. It's clear that she intended to cancel the deal before she was killed," Wes said as he folded his hands behind his back. "It's all settled. The important thing is that you are safe."

"Yes." Mary met her eyes. "Absolutely."

Paul's car screeched into the parking lot. Suzie looked up and felt her heart leap at the sight of him. It didn't matter to her that he might want to marry her, or that he had a ring hidden on his boat. All that mattered was that he was there. Suzie opened her arms to him. He pulled her close and held her against his chest until her trembling eased.

"I love you, Suzie."

"I love you too, Paul." She felt his muscles relax in response to her words. She tightened her arms around him. Maybe Paul had different ideas of where love should lead, but she was glad that he wanted to share that love with her.

Chapter Nineteen

After all the reports had been filed and medical evaluations completed, Suzie returned to Dune House with Mary and Paul at her side.

"I am exhausted." Mary yawned as soon as they walked in the door. "Do you want something to eat, Suzie? Some tea?"

"No Mary, the only thing I want is for you to rest." She hugged her friend. "Please?"

"All right, I won't argue." Mary smiled. "But no wandering off, okay?"

"I promise," Suzie said. As Mary walked down the hall to her room Paul rubbed Suzie's shoulders.

"I'm guessing you need to rest, too."

"Actually, I'm wired. I don't think I could sit still if I tried."

"Oh, good." Paul smiled and looked into her eyes. "Then how about a walk on the beach?"

Suzie started to nod in agreement, then she remembered the ring. "Oh uh, maybe in a little while. I think I see Jason pulling up." She hurried away from Paul and out onto the porch. Jason's patrol car parked. He stepped out, followed by Summer.

"Is something wrong, Jason?" Suzie frowned. Paul wrapped his arm around her shoulders.

"No, nothing is wrong."

"I insisted on making sure that you were okay." Summer searched Suzie for any visible injuries. "I needed to see for myself."

"I'm okay." Suzie laughed. "I still have all of my pieces and parts."

"Well, that's a relief." Summer sighed.

Paul nodded to Jason. "It's a beautiful day isn't it, Jason?"

"Yes." Jason met Paul's eyes. "It is."

"Some would say perfect." Paul lifted an eyebrow.

"You're right." Jason smiled. "It is perfect."

Suzie looked between the two as she tried to follow their conversation. She'd never known Paul and Jason to discuss the weather.

"So beautiful, we're going to take a walk on the beach, while Mary is resting. You two should stay. I'm sure you can find a perfect place for a perfect moment."

"Good idea." Jason grinned. "Enjoy your walk."

"Oh, but I should get them something to drink and eat." Suzie started to turn back towards the house. Paul held her close to him.

"No, we're going for a walk." He met her eyes. Paul was never one to command her. She wasn't sure what to think.

"I'm not sure that I'm up for a walk."

"Well, we need to talk." Paul tugged her towards the sand. Suzie's heart began to race. She was sure that Paul was trying to force the issue of the proposal. But she knew if she argued anymore things would become more awkward.

"Okay, sure." Suzie smiled at Jason and Summer. "Help yourself to anything you like."

"Thanks." Jason winked at Paul. There it was. Suzie was sure that they were plotting something. Paul escorted her away from Dune House. After a few feet he paused.

"Wait Suzie, here, stand here." He turned her to face the house.

"What? Why?"

"Please, just trust me." Paul kissed her cheek.

"Paul, wait, please don't." Suzie looked into his eyes.

"What is it, Suzie? What's wrong?" He took her hands in his.

"Paul, after everything I've gone through there's no question in my mind how much I love you."

"I love you, too, Suzie."

"But I don't want to get married, Paul. At least

249

not right now. I don't know if I ever want to. But if I did, it would be to you."

"Married? What are you talking about, Suzie?" Paul frowned.

"I'm sorry if I've hurt you. I hope that you still want to continue our relationship."

"You haven't hurt me. I know that you're not interested in that right now, and that's okay with me. A piece of paper wouldn't change how I feel about you. All that matters to me is that you are happy."

"Really?" Suzie's eyes widened. "But I don't understand. What about the ring?"

"The ring?" Paul raised an eyebrow. "Oh! The ring!" He grinned. "Never mind about that."

"What do you mean? Is it for someone else?"

"Yes, it is." He smiled.

"So, you're marrying someone else?" Suzie blinked back tears of panic that tried to rise to her eyes. "Is it because I won't?"

"No, I'm sorry, Suzie, I've confused you. The ring is for someone else, and it's from someone else."

"Now, I'm really confused."

"Just wait. I think that everything will become very clear to you soon."

"How?"

"Look over there." He pointed towards the deck of Dune House that overlooked the water.

Suzie looked in the direction that he pointed. She saw Jason and Summer who stood very close together. Jason took her hand in his, then lowered down onto one knee. Suzie gasped and covered her mouth with her hand. Paul squeezed her free hand. Jason produced the ring box from his pocket and lifted the lid. He held it up to Summer. Though Suzie was at a distance from the pair she was sure she detected a tremble in Jason's hand. She looked over at Paul with wide eyes. He winked at her. The two watched as Summer smiled and wept at the same time. Finally, she nodded and

251

Jason stood up to embrace her. Suzie felt as if she'd witnessed a very sacred moment between her young cousin and his future wife.

"Jason didn't want to buy it from the jewelry shop because Summer's friend works there and he was afraid she would tell Summer so he asked me to order the ring before I went out in the boat. Then I picked it up when I docked. I kept it because he didn't want Summer to accidently find it. I couldn't tell you or Mary because he was afraid that one of you might drop a hint. He wanted it to be a surprise so that he would get an honest answer. It looks like he got his answer."

"Yes, it does." Suzie tilted her head against his. "I'm so happy for him." Paul encircled her waist with his arms.

"I love you, Suzie. Whether you want to marry me or not, whether you want to live alone forever or not. Nothing will change the way I feel about you."

"I love you too, Paul." She turned in his arms

to face him. "You've made my life complete by being part of it. I don't need anything more than that."

"Then we'll just keep loving each other and see where we end up. Sound good?"

"Sounds perfect." Suzie sighed and snuggled close to him.

"Lucky Benita saved you," Paul said.

"Yes, that bird is just as special as Priscilla always knew she was." Suzie sighed. "I'm going to miss her when she goes back to Leanne."

"Shall we take that walk on the beach now?" Paul asked.

"I would love to." Suzie wrapped her arm around his and the two began to walk down the dune towards the water.

Garber would remain, as it always was, a place of tranquility and beauty.

The End

More Cozy Mysteries by Cindy Bell

Dune House Cozy Mysteries

Seaside Secrets

Boats and Bad Guys

Treasured History

Hidden Hideaways

Dodgy Dealings

Suspects and Surprises

Ruffled Feathers

Sage Gardens Cozy Mysteries

Birthdays Can Be Deadly

Money Can Be Deadly

Trust Can Be Deadly

Ties Can Be Deadly

Rocks Can Be Deadly

Jewelry Can Be Deadly

Made in United States
North Haven, CT
07 July 2024

54501150R00147